DOCTOR WHO
THE CELESTIAL TOYMAKER

DOCTOR WHO
THE CELESTIAL TOYMAKER

Based on the BBC television series by Brian Hayles by arrangement with the British Broadcasting Corporation

GERRY DAVIS
and
ALISON BINGEMAN

No 111
in the Doctor Who library

TARGET

A TARGET BOOK
published by
the Paperback Division of
W.H. ALLEN & CO. PLC

A Target Book
Published in 1986
By the Paperback Division of
W.H. Allen & Co. PLC
44 Hill Street, London W1X 8LB

First published in Great Britain by
W.H. Allen & Co. PLC 1986

The BBC producer of *The Celestial Toymaker* was Innes Lloyd,
the director was Bill Selars

Printed and bound in Great Britain by
Anchor Brendon Ltd, Tiptree, Essex

ISBN 0 426 20251 1

Contents

Foreword by Gerry Davis

I doubt if many television dramas have been created in situations of such tension and pressure as *The Celestial Toymaker*. One week before we went into rehearsal, the original script by Brian Hayles was vetoed by the BBC Head of Drama Serials, Gerald Savory. Savory had given permission for characters from his greatest stage success *George and Margaret* (Savory was a distinguished West End Playwright before his TV days) to be used in *The Celestial Toymaker*. He then changed his mind at the last moment.

The trouble was, however, that Innes Lloyd (Producer) and myself (Editor) had just taken over the *Doctor Who* series and there were no other completed episodes to throw in the breach. Also, director Bill Sellers had already cast the George and Margaret parts, and designer John Wood had created the sets. An immediate, almost total rewrite was called for but unfortunately, the writer, the late Brian Hayles, a busy and popular screenwriter, was contracted elsewhere and unable to help us.

Innes gently reminded me that this kind of emergency effort was what editors were paid for – so I got to work at home, dispatching pages to the studio every three hours. All that was left of the original script

– minus George and Margaret – was the character of the Toymaker, the Doctor (who was on holiday most of the series) and the trilogic game. So I had 'carte blanche'. I went back to the diabolic nursery suggested by the title and brought to life the clowns, the King and Queen of Hearts, Mrs Wiggs and Sergeant Rugg (from an old pantomime sketch), the sinister ballet dolls and the slyly wicked schoolboy Cyril (who was *not* meant to resemble Billy Bunter – just the capacity for mischief that exists in most schoolboys).

Happily, the middle-aged players already hired for the serial rose magnificently to the challenge of mime (clowns), slapstick (Mrs Wiggs and Sergeant Rugg), royalty (the Hearts) and managed to make the characters both sinister and touching at the same time.

For this book version we were able to resurrect some extra material which had to be cut from the TV serial and recreate the sets as originally envisaged, free from the restrictions imposed by the emergency we were in at the time of production.

Gerry Davis, Los Angeles, 1985

1

Trapped

'Doctor, you've vanished.'

Dodo and Steven stared with disbelief at the hexagonal control board of the TARDIS. A moment before, the Doctor had been standing there; now he seemed to have vanished into thin air.

'What? What nonsense! Nonsense, child.' The familiar, slightly crusty voice of the first Doctor echoed round the room. The Doctor's young companions smiled with relief.

'Thank goodness you're still there,' said Dodo.

'But is he?' Steven interjected. 'I can't see him.' Steven moved forward and waved his hand where the Doctor's voice had been coming from. It met with no obstacle. 'You seem to have dematerialised,' Steven continued.

'Extraordinary!' cried the Doctor's voice. 'One could say I only exist through the sound of my voice.'

'Do you think this is something to do with the Refusians?' queried Dodo anxiously, referring to the race of invisible aliens they had encountered on their previous journey.

'It must be,' Steven replied tersely.

'No!' came the Doctor's voice, 'You're wrong. This is something else much more serious. We are in grave danger. This must be some form of attack.'

Dodo and Steven looked anxiously at each other. 'But,' said Steven, 'we're still inside the TARDIS. Surely nothing can harm us inside here?'

'Evidently there is some great power that can penetrate beyond our safety barrier,' replied the Doctor's voice.

If the Doctor and his companions had been able to look outside (the scanner was not on) they would have been able to see that the TARDIS was standing in the middle of a large octagonal room, not unlike the interior of the TARDIS itself. From each angle, lines stretched to the centre of the room. The TARDIS was standing at the exact point where the lines intersected.

The room was painted white but seemed to have some sort of inner lumination, a kind of luminosity that radiated a soft incandescent glow. The only furniture visible was a simple short wooden bench facing one of the walls and, against the wall immediately behind the TARDIS, a wooden cupboard of a plain antique design. No-one was inside the room.

Inside the TARDIS, Steven and Dodo were still standing looking towards where they assumed the invisible Doctor to be.

'Don't just stand there.' The Doctor was now behind them. They both jumped and turned to the new location of the Doctor's voice. 'Tcha, tcha.' The others could almost see the Doctor's hand slapping the lapel of his coat, as he did when he was irritated by something. 'Come and turn on the scanner.'

'But Doctor, don't you think –' Dodo began.

'Don't ask questions,' said the Doctor. 'We may not

have time. Turn on the scanner now.'

Steven ran over to the control console and flicked on the scanner, then quickly looked up at it. The screen was completely blank.

'It doesn't show anything,' said Steven. 'It's not working.'

'Yes it is,' said the Doctor. 'When it isn't working the screen is distorted, now it's perfectly clear. This is obviously part of the same trick that brought us here.'

Dodo turned to the Doctor. 'What are we to do then, Doctor?' she asked. 'Let's take off at once.'

'That might be worse.' The Doctor's voice was moving across the room. 'Besides, I'm not only invisible, I'm also intangible, which means I can't pull the switches on the TARDIS.'

Steven stepped forward looking vainly around for the new location of the Doctor. 'I'll do that, Doctor, if you'll tell me what to do.'

'But Steven,' replied Dodo, 'if the Doctor is dematerialised and we take off now, he might never again regain his physical form.'

'You're quite right, Dodo. Whatever it is, we have to face it. Open the doors.'

Steven shook his head anxiously: 'But Doctor!'

The Doctor's voice came across imperiously, with that peculiar ring he used when he had decided upon a line of action. 'Open the doors!'

Steven turned back to the control console, put his hand forward and touched a control. The others heard the slight whir as the mechanism operated and the door opened.

'Now, you wait for me here,' the Doctor's voice came

11

to them as though moving across the room.

Steven and Dodo glanced at each other. Dodo shook her head: 'I really think we should go with him.'

'You heard what he said,' said Steven. 'And besides, how could we ever follow him?'

'I don't understand,' said Dodo. 'If the Doctor's intangible then why does he need to open the doors? He could have just as easily walked through them.'

Steven walked over to the door and glanced out. 'Habit, I suppose,' he said over his shoulder. Then he turned back to Dodo. 'It looks quite safe out there; I think we should inspect.'

Dodo shook her head firmly. 'You won't get me out there.'

Inside his ornate study, the Celestial Toymaker, the being who had captured the TARDIS and its inhabitants, was surveying his extraordinary kingdom. The Toymaker's study appeared at first like a room. Then, as you became accustomed to its dimensions, you realised that instead of a roof there was a black immensity of outer space and the twinkling stars of the galaxies. The walls stretched up towards the blackness until they became indistinguishable from space and merged with it.

Hanging on the walls was every conceivable type of toy: mechanical toys, electronic toys, dolls, teddy bears, puppets, marionettes and masks, some friendly and smiling, glittering with a malevolent presence of their own. Scattered around the floor of the panelled, eighteenth-century room were a series of antique tables:

upon each of them stood a doll's house or marionette theatre. Some tables held various types of games, ranging from pinball machines to chess, to obscure board games dating back over the centuries, many of which had long since been forgotten in the mists of time.

The Toymaker was lounging in a black Chinese chair behind a laquered Chinese desk inlaid with mother-of-pearl and scenes of Chinese life, after the style of the Willow pattern.

Further around the room there was a collection of mechanical clocks: some with figurines which came out and struck the hour with huge gongs; some, like the ancient town clocks of medieval Germany with a series of figures led by Father Time with his scythe that paraded when the hour was struck. The whirring clicking mechanisms, the occasional cuckoo from the cuckoo clocks and the loud ticking from the grandfather clocks produced an almost symphonic medley of sound.

Incongruously, the antique desk possessed a series of switches and buttons glowing softly with a carefully coded system of vari-coloured lights. In front of the desk stood a triangular table with the letters A, B and C inlaid in each corner. On two sides of the table, there were two chairs.

The Toymaker stood up, a tall imposing figure, dressed as a Chinese mandarin with a circular black hat embossed with heavy gold thread, a large silver red and blue collar and a heavy, stiffly embroidered black robe encrusted with rubies, emeralds, diamonds and pearls set against a background of coiled Chinese dragons.

With a wave of his hand the Toymaker stopped the cacophony of ticking, clicking machines. He looked

13

around the room with his deep-set glittering eyes. 'Let's see now,' he said, 'I think it's time to play a few games.' The Toymaker smoothly walked over to the first doll's house, a large Victorian one, each room of which was furnished in meticulous detail with tiny furniture, carpets, chandeliers and curtains. Inside sat a collection of small Victorian dolls dressed in the stiff formal clothes of the period.

The Toymaker's long slender fingers flickered over them for a moment while he considered, then he passed on to the first of the toy theatres. He bent forward and pulled a thin cord at the side, opening the large embroidered curtains. Inside there was a circus ring with bleachers rising up from the circular floor, each with a tiny figure smiling at the antics of the two clowns.

'Yes,' said the Toymaker, 'I think you two will serve my purpose admirably. You are very good at games: clowns always are. You can throw Steven and Dodo a few of your tricks into the bargain.'

The Toymaker reached in and drew out the two clown dolls, one in each hand. One was a girl doll dressed in a baggy harlequin, one-piece costume with a diamond pattern, a thick neck ruff and silk stockings. Her face was stretched in a wide and inviting smile. Her nose was tipped with scarlet, her eyes wide open as if in wonderment at the world; her hair swept up in the clown's traditional three peaks ending in curled points.

By contrast, the male clown was a sad-looking fellow. Unlike his companion, all the lines in his face turned downward ... from his long lugubrious mouth to his red-rimmed, sad clown's eyes. He was dressed in a clown's costume, a white baggy suit and ruffles edged

14

with blue on his wrists and neck. On his head he had a cone-shaped clown hat with a blue band.

The Toymaker carefully put the two clowns down onto the floor and raised his left hand. On his middle finger, a large sapphire ring began to flash as he pointed his hand towards the two clowns. Concentric rings of blue fire appeared – flashing down and surrounding the dolls who immediately began to grow, larger and larger; until confronting the Toymaker, were two life size clowns. Each made him a comic bow.

The Toymaker smiled at his creations. 'Yes,' he said, 'I think you'll do.'

Meanwhile, Steven and Dodo were having a fierce argument. 'I don't know why you always have to be so obstinate,' said Dodo stamping her feet impatiently. 'The Doctor asked us to wait here.'

'But he hasn't returned,' replied Steven hotly. 'I'm going out there to look for him.'

Steven stepped outside the shelter of the TARDIS into the room and called, 'Doctor, Doctor.' Timidly, Dodo stepped out beside him.

'What is it?' The Doctor's voice was loud. They jumped and turned. There he was, visible and his old self again.

'I can see you,' said Steven.

'Everything must be all right then,' chimed in Dodo.

The Doctor looked down at his hands. 'Ah, you can see me.'

'It doesn't seem too bad here,' said Dodo looking around the room.

'It's a strange-looking place,' agreed Steven. 'Have you ever seen it before?'

'I'm not sure,' the Doctor shook his head. 'There is something about it that is very familiar.'

Dodo completed her inspection of the room with its bare white walls and two articles of furniture. 'It looks dead boring to me. Come on.' She turned back to the TARDIS.

'Wait, child,' said the Doctor, reaching out for Dodo's arm.

'Why?' said Dodo with the obstinacy of someone with her mind made up.

'Well, I don't think that it was the Refusian influence which made me intangible.' The Doctor clutched his lapels and threw his head back in a familiar gesture. 'No, there is something here that I feel is important to me – to us. I don't like the feel of the place any more than you, but I think someone, or something, willed us to come here and we must face whatever happens.'

Steven, meanwhile, was gazing with fixed intensity at the wall. 'Look there,' said Steven. 'It's me!'

Dodo peered over at the wall following Steven's gaze. She saw nothing: the wall was white and blank. 'I don't see anything there,' she said.

'But you must,' said Steven, 'Look!' As Steven watched he saw himself clad in Elizabethan type clothes, with a slashed doublet, thigh length boots and carrying a long rapier in his hand. 'It's me,' he said, 'Look, Doctor,' he called. 'We're back in the Massacre of Saint Bartholomew in Paris.'

The Doctor who had been examining the cupboard in the corner turned around and glanced over. Like Dodo, he only saw a blank wall in front of Steven and realised instantly what it was. 'Don't look at it, Steven! Now I know where we are.'

But his advice fell on deaf ears. 'It's changed, Doctor. We're on the Space Ark, remember? Look there – the Monoids.' As Steven watched he saw a screen filled with the monsters he had battled on the Space Ark carrying the survivors of a destroyed Earth to a new planet. The Monoids were hideous shaggy beings with one eye in the middle of their heads.

The Doctor became more insistent, marched over and pulled Steven away from the wall. 'Turn away this instant!' he said. 'I told you I know where we are. We are in the world of the Celestial Toymaker and this screen is hypnotic. He is trying to dominate your mind. Don't look whatever you do.'

Confused, Steven raised his hand to his brow. 'But Doctor,' he said, 'it looked so real.'

'There is *nothing* there,' the Doctor repeated. 'Nothing at all. You must believe me.'

'What's the matter, Doctor?' Dodo chipped in. 'I couldn't see anything on the screen. I can't even see a screen.' She walked over and suddenly started back in amazement. 'I thought I saw something!'

'No,' said the Doctor, 'you didn't. Turn away quickly.'

Dodo obediently turned towards the Doctor. 'Who is the Celestial Toymaker?' she queried.

'A powerful evil.' The Doctor's face darkened. 'He has created a universe entirely in his own vision, where he manipulates people and turns them into his playthings. He gains control of your mind through these

17

screens. Be careful, it's a trap.'

'Really, Doctor.' The Toymaker's laugh was low and musical. The Doctor and his companions turned. There standing facing them was the tall, imposing figure of the Celestial Toymaker.

'What a spoilsport you are, Doctor. I thought they would enjoy my memory window.'

'Look where he's standing,' said Steven. 'Isn't that ...'

'Yes!' Dodo echoed. They both looked around. The TARDIS had disappeared; the Toymaker was standing at the apex of the lines in place of the TARDIS.

'What have you done with the TARDIS?' cried Dodo.

'Don't worry my dear, just watch over there.' Almost hypnotised, Dodo turned to look at the nearest wall, unnoticed by the Doctor and Steven who were both caught up in the powerful hypnotic presence of the Toymaker.

'I suppose I should have guessed it was you when I realised the power of the force field you put around the TARDIS,' said the Doctor.

The Toymaker nodded slowly, an ironical smile on his face. 'Of course, Doctor. I have been waiting for you for such a long time.'

Dodo stared at the wall, which gradually became a screen and then resolved itself into a three-dimensional picture of an English living room. Dodo looked forward excitedly, 'It's home!' she said. 'And that's ...' Her face suddenly fell. A man was coming towards her from the screen. He shook his head sadly and Dodo realised that also standing in front of her was her younger self dressed in British school uniform: black stockings, gymslip and beret. As Dodo watched, her younger self turned away in tears and hid her face.

'It's me,' Dodo's voice became choked with emotion. 'It's the day my mother died. That's awful!'

The Doctor, suddenly realising what had happened, turned abruptly. 'Come away, child, this instant!'

Steven ran over to Dodo and, seeing she was unable to drag herself away, swung her around. As he did so, the picture faded and Dodo buried her face in Steven's shoulder.

'What a shame,' the Toymaker's smooth deep tones cut in. 'I thought my little invention would amuse them and juggle their memories.'

'Your inventions are evil like yourself,' the Doctor sharply rejoined. He turned back to Steven and Dodo. 'You must be very careful. Everything here contains a hidden menace. Nothing is just for fun.'

Steven looked at the Doctor, being careful not to glance at the many walls around the room. 'What's the idea of it?'

'He is trying to get us in his power and make us a permanent fixture in his universe,' said the Doctor. 'That's the reason for those wall screens. He's using your mind and imagination against you. Those are memory devices that project difficult and upsetting times in your previous lives. You must fight it.'

Dodo looked up and pushed away from Steven. 'Can't we just go? I hate this place,' she said.

'How, my child?' The Doctor shrugged. 'That's the question.'

'In the TARDIS, of course. As always,' said Dodo.

19

Once more the Toymaker, who had kept silent through this exchange merely glancing from face to face with his hooded snake eyes, interjected. 'Ah, but *which* TARDIS? Take your choice.'

The Toymaker slowly stretched his arm out. The ring on his finger again began to pulsate and the circles of light began moving towards the wall. As the Doctor and his companions watched, they saw the wall begin to change colour and vibrate; then it slowly resolved into a picture of an endless conveyor belt of TARDIS police boxes slowly moving by them.

Steven shook his head in confusion. 'There are hundreds of them.'

'Yes,' said the Toymaker, 'hundreds. Take your choice. Come, Doctor.'

'No!' said the Doctor sharply.

Steven and Dodo tore their eyes away from the wall and turned back, but the Doctor and the Toymaker had both disappeared and the room was completely empty.

2

Bring On The Clowns

Steven and Dodo looked at each other, filled with a new sense of dread – first they had lost the TARDIS, and now the Doctor.

'Doctor,' Steven called.

'Have you gone invisible again?' Dodo echoed.

They listened for the Doctor's voice. Then Steven shook his head: 'He's gone this time. That mandarin or whoever he is has spirited him away somewhere.'

Dodo looked despondent. 'I don't like it,' she said. 'We should never have stayed. We should have got back in the TARDIS while the going was good.

'I don't think it would have helped,' said Steven. 'Anyway it's too late now.'

'Who was that man?' said Dodo.

Again Steven shook his head, 'I don't know, but we've got to find the Doctor.'

Steven glanced quickly around the room but none of the walls was illuminated. He pointed to the cupboard. 'Perhaps there's a way out through that cupboard over there,' he said.

They moved towards the cupboard and just as Steven stretched his arm out, the door was flung open. A clown's head appeared around the corner – the male clown.

Further down appeared the red-headed smiling face of the female clown. 'I'm Clara,' she said. The two clowns stepped out of the cupboard and looked around the room, miming wonderment mixed with a little anxiety.

'What on earth ...' Steven began. But the clowns immediately stopped and put their fingers to their mouths.

'Shh' said Clara. 'Shush' said Joey.

'Better keep quiet, Steven,' Dodo whispered.

Steven, belligerent as ever, squared his shoulders. He didn't like being told what to do even by the Doctor, but especially not from a couple of silly-looking clowns.

'I will not!' he began, then paused as Joey suddenly extended his hand out towards him. Dodo, irritated as she often was by Steven's tough guy attitude, moved away from him a little sulkily. Clara put her finger to her lips and brought a hand from behind her back revealing a large balloon and a hat pin; unseen by Steven who was looking suspiciously at the clown with his proffered hand.

Clara, a figure of fun and mischief, pantomimed to Dodo not to say anything and then knelt behind Steven. Dodo's face cleared – these were funny clowns. She stifled a giggle. Steven finally decided that the clown did not offer much of a threat. 'Hello then,' he said a little sulkily, and reached to take the clown's hand in his.

As Steven shook Joey's hand, the clown backed away leaving his hand in Steven's. It came away and stretched to a three or four foot long false arm.

Steven threw it down in disgust just as Clara stuck the pin into the balloon behind him. As Joey gave him a

22

little push, he jumped back nervously, falling over Clara.

The expression on Steven's face was too much for Dodo. After all the tension, she was ready for a laugh, and laugh she did at his furious face looking up at them. The clowns also held their sides and mimed convulsive laughter.

Gulping, Dodo said, 'If you could only see your face.' She laughed again.

Steven scowled up at her and then scrambled to his feet. 'Very funny,' he said, dusting his trousers off. 'What have you got to laugh about?' 'Oh, come on, Steven,' said Dodo still gasping for breath. 'If you could see it from my angle you'd think it was pretty funny too.'

She felt a tap on her shoulder and turned. Joey was holding a large bunch of flowers. He raised them to his nostrils and did an elaborate pantomime of smelling the fresh scents of the flowers. Then he made an elaborate bow and slowly presented her with the bouquet.

Dodo gazed in wonderment: there were roses and carnations, irises and some flowers she didn't even recognise – a magnificent bouquet. Her eyes widened.

'They're not for me?' she said. She looked at Joey who gravely nodded his head. Then she looked at Clara, her face fixed in her usual smile, who nodded and gave a curtsey.

'Oh,' said Dodo, 'I can't thank you enough. They're just beautiful. No-one has ever given me flowers before.'

She stretched out her hand, took the bouquet from Joey and raised them to her face. As she grasped the stalks, a strong jet of water sprung out into her face and

23

hair, saturating her.

Dodo stepped back and dropped the flowers. Steven's loud laugh rang out in the room. 'If you could only see your face!' he mimicked in Dodo's high-pitched voice. 'We need a laugh, don't we?' The sight of Dodo's woe-begone face was too much for him and he turned away, laughing.

Dodo reached in her pocket and brought out a handkerchief and started mopping herself. 'That's not funny at all.'

'Oh, but it was,' said Steven, still laughing.

'I'm not at all sure I like these clowns,' said Dodo. Steven turned to the clowns who had been pointing at Dodo and mimicking silent laughter again.

'Can't either of you speak?' said Steven. He turned to Joey. Joey pressed a button on his clown costume which made a slightly raucous sound which could have been a raspberry.

Steven turned to the other clown: 'How about you?'

Clara's mouth suddenly opened, giving out a high-pitched voice that started low and rose up the scale.

'Yes,' she squeaked, 'I can talk, I can say lots of things. Once you get me started I can't stop. I can talk about –'

'Right, right,' said Steven cutting in, 'that's enough.' He looked from one to the other. 'Look,' he said. 'What do you two want with us?'

The smooth mellow tones of the Toymaker echoed behind Steven: 'They've come to entertain you both. To play a game with you.'

Steven and Dodo wheeled and backed slightly away from the tall, thin-faced Toymaker. 'Thanks very much,' said Steven dryly. 'We've been entertained, and we're not in the mood for any other games right now. Perhaps you'll tell us where you have taken the Doctor.'

'Taken the Doctor?' said the Toymaker silkily, his voice taking on an ironic edge. 'Nowhere! The Doctor and I have to play a little game together. You can follow the results on that board.'

The Toymaker turned and pointed to one of the walls just as a robot appeared. Again the Toymaker raised his hand and the robot slowly came forward towards them. It was a large featureless black robot with arms and legs and, in place of a chest unit was a large monitor screen; it had flashing lights for eyes.

'If you watch that board,' said the Toymaker, 'you will see the results of a little game the Doctor and I will play together. It's called the trilogic game. I'm sure the Doctor will be a worthy opponent.'

Dodo turned to him angrily, 'We're not interested in your silly games, we want to go back to the TARDIS.'

The Toymaker smiled and slowly shook his head. 'Not quite yet, my young friends.' He pointed. Over behind them the clowns had been bringing a series of objects out from the cupboard as if setting up for a children's game. 'I'm afraid you cannot go back to the TARDIS yet, it's impossible.'

'Impossible?' Steven and Dodo spoke together.

Again the Toymaker smiled his cat-like smile. 'Well, not quite impossible. But you'll have to win a few games first. At the end of each game you'll find a TARDIS which may or may not be the real one.'

Steven looked at him. 'What do you mean, the real one?'

'Oh, you'll find out when you open the door,' he said. 'As you have already noticed, I have many copies of the TARDIS around.'

'Are you saying,' Dodo came forward a pace, 'we have to win a game before we can get to the TARDIS?'

The Toymaker nodded. 'Yes. Several games, in fact.'

'And if we lose?' said Steven.

Again, the Toymaker smiled and folded his arms in a classic Mandarin pose. 'You will both stay here forever as my guests.'

Dodo looked at Steven. 'I think we'd better play this silly game, Steven,' she said.

Steven shook his head angrily. 'I don't see why we should humour him. He must be crazy.'

'That's just it. I'm sure he *is* crazy,' said Dodo. 'But we'd better do as he says, otherwise we'll never get out.

They turned back to where the Toymaker had been watching this little exchange with his usual amused smile. 'Well?' he said.

Steven nodded reluctantly. 'We'll play your little games. If we win, we get the TARDIS back, okay?'

'But of course,' the Toymaker rejoined.

'And if we lose?' said Steven.

'That would be too bad,' said the Toymaker. 'You will never see the TARDIS again.'

'Wait a minute –' Steven stepped forward angrily but the Toymaker slowly vanished.

Dodo grasped his arm. 'You never asked him about the Doctor.'

'I suppose he's got this game to play,' said Steven. 'This I don't understand, I'm glad we're not playing it. It looks very complicated.' Steven walked over and studied the monitor on the robot which showed the triangular board marked *A*, *B* and *C*. In each corner there was a pile of triangular counters piled up like three pyramids.

'Then what are we playing?' asked Dodo. 'I don't understand.' The two clowns came up to them and they noticed that the clowns had set up a series of obstacles around the room. 'Look what they've done,' said Dodo.

Dodo and Steven looked around in astonishment. During their short talk with the Toymaker, the clowns had performed a seeming miracle.

The room now resembled a cross between a gymnasium and an army training obstacle course. There were two ropes slung over a number of sharp pointed iron spikes. A series of stepping stones were placed on something that looked like a carpet; a long thin plank was mounted over two sets of step ladders; and a long caterpillar-like tube snaked across the room and ended up at a square marked 'Home'. The floor itself seemed to have taken on the aspect of a large playing board.

'It's Snakes and Ladders!' cried Dodo. 'Doesn't it look like Snakes and Ladders, Steven. I had a set once that looked exactly like that.'

'It looks crazy and more than a little dangerous to me,' said Steven.

'Oh, I don't know,' said Dodo. 'It looks rather fun. I'd like to play it.'

Clara, overhearing Dodo's voice, turned to her and beckoned her towards a glass booth standing in a corner of the room. 'You play from there,' said the female clown. She pointed to Steven. 'He plays the actual game.' Then she lent forward and in a loud comical whisper said, 'That's because he's got the brawn and you've got the brains.'

Dodo couldn't help laughing, especially on catching sight of Steven's disgusted expression. 'Forget it,' he said. 'Me play on that? Not on your life.'

'Oh,' said Dodo disappointed. 'But this is the game we have to play in order to get back the TARDIS isn't it?'

Clara nodded. 'This is your game. If you lose it you'll never see your police box again.' She looked across at Joey whose face was set in an even more miserable expression than ever. The clowns turned back to Steven and Dodo and nodded together.

The Doctor and the Toymaker, meanwhile, were standing in the Toymaker's private office. The Doctor was examining the cluster of gleaming hi-tech toys which were suspended from the end of the room. All were deadly weapons of destruction. There was a model of an advanced missile complete with a deadly warhead, made to scale with exact measurements. Next to it was the long gleaming black hull of a nuclear submarine. Above it, the thin elegant dart shape of a supersonic bomber.

'You see, Doctor,' said the Toymaker. 'I'm not the only one who likes to play with expensive toys. On Earth, these are considered the most expensive toys of all. Expensive, because they are made solely to be played with, and never to be used.'

'Pshaw,' said the Doctor irritably. 'I'm not the slightest bit interested in your toy collection. Kindly cease this practical joking and let us go at once.'

The Toymaker turned back and smiled ironically, then walked over to his desk, sat down and leant back, placing his fingertips together and looking at the Doctor through the tops of his fingers. 'Patience Doctor, patience. You have only just got here, now relax. It's so very nice to see you again.'

The Doctor came up, stood in front of the desk and slowly turned around. 'Now,' he said with a rare flash of humour, 'you've seen me, so let us go.'

The Toymaker laughed. 'I'm glad you haven't lost your sense of humour, Doctor. I think you're going to need it.'

'What do you mean?' said the Doctor.

'Please sit down,' said the Toymaker. As the Doctor sat opposite him, the Toymaker continued. 'The last time you were here, I'd hoped you'd stay for a game or two, but you hardly gave me the time of day before you took off again.'

The Doctor stared at him. 'And very wise I was too.' The Doctor slapped his lapels in irritation. 'And you've been conniving ever since to bring me and my companions back here. You and your games are notorious throughout the universe. You draw people to this place like a spider attracts flies. Then you enmesh them in this devilish web of yours and they never get away again.'

'My games, notorious!' replied the Toymaker. 'Really Doctor, you are quite wrong.' The Toymaker motioned to his elaborate office: 'This is my universe. All I expect people to do is to play games to amuse themselves. It also amuses me to see them play. There is no web to enmesh them. If they continue to play throughout eternity, perhaps they were – how shall I say? – fated to do so.'

'Fate?' The Doctor paused for a moment then leant forward and picked up a small, perfectly made model of an astronaut off the Toymaker's desk and stared down at it suspiciously. 'I suspect this fellow was one of your victims of fate. Was *he* amused by your games?'

The Toymaker's eyes flicked over towards the small astronaut doll. He shrugged. 'Perhaps he was, Doctor but then he lost the game, you see, and became one of my toys.' The Toymaker reached over, took the doll from the Doctor's hand and put it back on the desk. 'But, like all my dolls, he will have a chance to play another game and regain his human form. Surely this is what life is all about. We all play games, even you, Doctor.'

'Your universe, Toymaker, has blinded you to reality. Everything is not predetermined according to your desires. Humans do have free will.' The Doctor leant back, crossed his arms and shook his head obstinately. 'I refuse to play your games,' he said.

'But you are here now, Doctor, and subject to my will,' replied the Toymaker. 'I have a doll's house hanging over there which should be just right for you. It's full of furniture that exactly matches the period of your clothes; Victorian, I think.'

The Doctor stared back at him. 'I should never have come out of the TARDIS,' he said.

'But you're insatiably curious, Doctor,' said the Toymaker. 'That's why I ensured that the scanner should be blank. I knew that would make you come outside. Besides, if you had taken off immediately, you might have remained forever invisible.' At the thought, the Toymaker threw back his head and laughed.

The two ancient enemies locked glances across the desk for a long moment. Finally the Doctor nodded slowly in acknowledgement: the Toymaker had won the first round. 'What game do you want me to play?' asked the Doctor.

The Toymaker smiled. 'At last,' he said. 'Here, Doctor.' He rose, turned, and gestured over towards the table on which stood the trilogic game. He waved his hand and the three piles resolved into one big pyramid. Each segment of the pyramid from the tiny cone at the top to the largest segment at the bottom was numbered. 'All you have to do Doctor is to reassemble these segments in the same order they are now, on point C. He pointed to one of the three triangles of the game.

Interested despite himself, the Doctor stared at the board and quickly calculated. 'I'm only allowed to move one piece at a time right?' he said.

The Toymaker nodded. 'That's right.'

'And I'm never permitted to put a larger piece on a smaller one?' said the Doctor, pleased as always when his sometimes fallible memory worked efficiently.

'Absolutely correct,' said the Toymaker. 'And you have 1023 moves to do it in, and that is the exact amount, mind you – no more or less. If you make one mistake – you lose!' He crossed back to the desk and pushed a lever. At the far side of the table, there was a tally recorder with two lines of figures. 'This is to help you count. The top line shows 1023 moves. As you progress, the bottom will record the moves you make.

31

When the two lines match, the game is over.'

The Doctor raised his head, intrigued by the challenge the game presented. 'I see,' he said. 'Can I begin?'

'Wait,' said the Toymaker. 'Don't be too impatient. Look at this.' The Toymaker touched another button at his desk and waved his hand at a large ornate mirror hanging along with the other objects behind the desk. The mirror turned cloudy and then gradually resolved into a picture of Steven, Dodo and the clowns in the other room. 'Don't forget your companions,' he said.

The Doctor sniffed. 'You aren't going to make them play this game are you?'

'Good heavens, no,' said the Toymaker with a hint of condescension. 'This would be much too difficult for Steven and Dodo. They're on a competitive quest.'

'Tcha, tcha,' said the Doctor. 'You don't make sense, man. Competitive quest? What do you mean? And who are those others with them!'

The Toymaker pointed over to the screen. 'Those are two clown friends of mine. They're what we could call the home team. They're going to play against your friends and win the quest.' Again, the Toymaker laughed.

'I don't understand you,' said the Doctor irritably. 'Quest? What quest?'

The Toymaker waved his hand at the screen again before answering. Again the picture defocused and gradually resolved to a picture of the TARDIS, 'The quest for your interesting little spacecraft,' he said. 'The TARDIS. All you have to do is win the games and you can have it back, Doctor. But you must both win the games at exactly the same time.' So you will have to pace your' – the Toymaker bowed slightly – 'brilliant playing with the lesser efforts of your friends.'

Stunned by the Toymaker's sarcasm, the Doctor raised his finger and snapped it in a derisive gesture. 'You couldn't vanquish me last time, and you won't vanquish me this time,' he said. 'Nor my friends. They will beat your clowns or anyone else you send against them, just as I will master this trifling game of yours.'

The Doctor turned back to the table and sat down at the chair opposite the counters, hoping that the Toymaker could not read the slightly anxious set of his frown. The Doctor and his companions were really up against it this time. He only hoped Steven and Dodo were as aware of the danger as he was.

3

Snakes and Ladders

Meanwhile in the Toyroom, the clown Clara was explaining the rules of the game to Steven and Dodo. 'You start here blindfolded. It's really very simple,' said the clown. 'You have to cross these obstacles safely without falling.'

Steven pointed over to the male clown with the sad face. 'What's whatever his name going to be doing all this time?' he asked.

'His name is Joey,' said Clara. 'And I'm Clara. He will do it too, of course.'

'And if he loses?' queried Steven. Clara turned away. Steven turned back to Dodo. 'No answer that time. Well, suppose we both manage it?'

'Then we do it again,' said Clara. 'Until someone loses.'

'Yes,' said Steven. 'Great future the Toymaker's mapped out for us! Okay, chum, you want to show us how it's done?' He turned to Joey who was just putting the finishing touches to the course. Joey nodded his head, beeped on a horn which he carried at his waist and rang a little bell.

Steven raised his eyelids a little wearily. 'That means yes, I suppose?' Again Joey honked his horn while Clara tied a blindfold over the clown's eyes. Then she turned to Dodo.

'You must come with me,' she said. 'You can come too, Steven.' She led the way across to the glass booth in the corner of the Toyroom. Inside was a simple control desk and a large red button.

'This is the buzzer button,' she indicated. 'One buzz for right turn, two for left, three for stop, four for start.' Clara pressed the buzzer four times.

As Steven and Dodo watched, they saw Joey feel for the rope, untie it and swing across the sharp spikes, expertly feeling for and landing on the first stepping-stone. He then started striding confidently across the remaining stepping-stones.

'Well, if that's all there is to it,' said Steven, 'any clown can do it.' He turned around expectantly, waiting for a ripple of laughter or at least a glimmer of appreciation for one of his rare jokes. But neither Clara nor Joey even giggled. Steven shrugged, regaining his offhand manner. 'Well,' he said. 'There's certainly nothing there that I can't manage to do. When do I start?' He looked to Clara.

Inside the Toymaker's study, the Doctor was watching Dodo and Steven intently on the monitor. Now he walked quickly over to the Toymaker's desk and searched for the inter-communication button that linked the Toymaker with the Toyroom. He pressed it, leant forward and spoke urgently through the desk microphone. 'Steven! Dodo! Listen to me: be very careful how you play this game. It's not as innocent as it looks. So be on your guard. Watch out for –' the Doctor went on ... but there was a click behind him and he realised that he was talking into a dead microphone.

Whirling around he saw the Toymaker suddenly materialise by the desk. 'That was unwise of you, Doctor.' The Toymaker sounded serious.

The Doctor confronted him. 'I must warn them.'

'No,' said the Toymaker. 'You'd better attend to your own game. Go for move 152.'

On the trilogic board, the pieces started moving of their own volition. The counter number went up from 110 to 152. 'Keep playing,' said the Toymaker. 'And to stop you from interfering further, I shall have to dematerialise you again. Like this.' The Toymaker waved his arm and the Doctor faded from sight.

The Doctor's voice rang out across the study as if to compensate for his lack of visible presence. 'You are overreaching yourself, Toymaker,' he said. 'How can I play this game of yours?'

The Toymaker considered for an instant then nodded. 'Let's see. I think if we left you one hand ...' He snapped his fingers and the Doctor's hand with his distinctive ring materialised over the board. 'There now,' continued the Toymaker, 'I suggest you resume the game if you are to win back the TARDIS.'

There was a moment's pause and then the hand with great dignity picked up a piece from one section of the board and placed it on another.

'I thought you'd see it my way Doctor.' The Toymaker's voice was almost a purr.

In the Toyroom, Joey had just reached the end of the

tube, and as he crawled out, he felt the end of the square marked 'Home' and stood up. At once, a light came on and flashed, reading *HOME*. He raised his hand, whipped the blindfold off and clasped his hands in the air in a gesture of victory. 'We've won,' said Clara. 'We've won!'

'Hey,' said Steven. 'Not yet you haven't. I haven't had a go.'

Dodo looked up. 'The Doctor was trying to warn us about something Steven.'

'There's nothing to be afraid of,' Steven countered. 'I can do it. Now, let's see. Rope, swing across, five stepping-stones, and up and onto the plank, across the plank and then down and into the tube. It's a piece of cake,' he said and turned to Dodo. 'Just as long as you guide me. After all, if he can do it, I can. Now remember the signals and make sure you get them right.'

Dodo frowned at him. She didn't like it when Steven treated her like a child, as if she wasn't responsible. She was a good deal more responsible than he was most of the time, she thought. Steven went for things with the single-mindedness of a bull – he was a good-hearted fellow and would do anything for anybody, but he also caused trouble by, as the Doctor put it, bashing in before considering the situation carefully enough.

'All right, don't forget,' said Dodo. 'One buzz for right, two for left, four to start, and three to stop,' she illustrated her words by giving a demonstration with the buttons as she talked.

'Good girl,' said Steven a little patronisingly. He left the booth and walked out onto the floor. Clara followed him and tied the blindfold round his head.

'Can you see anything?' she asked.

Steven tried to look around but the blindfold was tied very tightly. All he could see was blackness. 'Not a thing,' he said. He felt round for the end of the rope and grasped it. 'Right,' he said. 'I'm ready!'

Clara went back to the booth and closed the door. She turned to Dodo. 'Start him off,' she said. Dodo pressed her finger on the buzzer and gave four loud, long buzzes.

Steven grasped the rope and then, testing it with both arms, he prepared to swing. To her horror, Dodo saw Joey walk over to the first stepping-stone and, while pretending to make sure it was safe, move it about a foot to the right.

'Look what he's doing! Cheat, cheat!' she shouted. 'Steven look out!'

Clara tittered. 'He can't hear you.' Dodo ran to the door of the booth and tried it. 'And the door is self-locking.' Dodo looked around desperately and ran back to the control panel. She buzzed three times.

Out on the floor, Steven, just about to swing across, almost overbalanced as he heard the buzzers. He recovered just in time and shouted, 'Dodo what are you doing? You nearly made me fall that time!' There was no answer from Dodo so he once more grasped the rope and launched off to swing across the sharp pointed spikes. Lowering his feet on the other side where he expected to find the stone – he found nothing! – and swung back again like some jungle creature. He lowered his feet to safety at the starting point.

'What have you done?' he said angrily. 'It must be you, you wretched clown!' For answer, Joey only honked at him. Then Dodo buzzed once.

Steven thought for a moment. 'Now, let's see: one buzz means go to the right. Well, let's try.' He grasped hold of the rope, flexed his muscles, pulled himself up and swung again in a large arc right across the waiting pinnacle of steel below.

This time, as he swung more to the right, he extended a leg and just found the edge of the stepping-stone. Quickly, with the agility of a born athlete, Steven released the rope and landed a little unsteadily onto the stepping-stone. 'Phew, that was close.' Once more, behind him, Joey honked on the horn.

'Yeah,' said Steven. 'You'll honk from the other side of your mouth once I get this blindfold off.' He started to gingerly stretch his leg out, feeling for the next stepping-stone.

Once more Joey, pretending to be nonchalant, kicked another of the stepping-stones out of the way.

Steven, having memorised the position of the stepping-stones, commenced his obstacle race, and stepped onto the second stepping-stone. 'Good,' he said. 'Now, the next one is, let me see, turn left.'

Dodo's buzzer began to sound: one, two, three. 'Oh no,' he said, 'what now?' This time, Dodo buzzed just once. 'To the right again?' said Steven. Joey honked in the background. 'You just wait,' he said. Steven extended his foot but couldn't find the stepping-stone. He tried once more, almost overbalancing, and finally found the step.

Again, Dodo buzzed just once. Steven repeated a step to the right and the final one to the left. He felt for the steps leading up to the plank, found them, and sat down on the lower step, wiping his brow.

Dodo was angry. 'I don't see how we will have a chance at winning when you cheat all the time,' she said to Clara.

Clara tittered. 'Cheat? No, we don't cheat. A few harmless variations makes it more fun, don't you think?' Clara reached over and removed a hard-boiled egg from Dodo's ear. 'Perhaps you need something to eat?' she said. 'Here.'

Dodo flung it down on the floor in disgust. The egg bounced back off the floor and hit her square in the forehead. Clara burst out in a gale of giggles. Dodo stamped her foot, infuriated. 'I don't think I like clowns anymore,' she said and turned back, wiping her brow, to watch Steven's progress. Perhaps he was doing better than she.

Through the glass booth she could see that Steven had climbed up to the top of the steps. Then she saw that Joey was leaning against the further set of steps and manicuring his nails with a gigantic nail file.

'What's he doing?' Dodo said, no longer trusting the slightest gesture of the clowns.

'Isn't it obvious?' she said, not waiting for a reply. 'He's manicuring his nails. And it's about time too.'

Steven reached the top of the steps and, stretching forth a leg, cautiously felt for the plank. He tested it carefully, feeling it give under his weight. Then, bringing his other foot up, started to edge along it towards the other end. As he inched forward leaving the safety of the first set of steps, he began to regain his old confidence. He stepped out a little more vigorously.

Beep! went the loud honk of Joey's horn. Steven swayed to and fro on the narrow plank, desperately fighting for his balance. Gradually, he righted himself. 'What on earth was that?' he called. Again he heard Joey honking his horn. 'Not you again!' he cried. 'I warn you!'

Joey reached down to press the top button on his tunic. A low vulgar raspberry sound came out. Steven, furious, swayed again – nearly falling off, and he began swinging his arms back to keep his balance. He stopped and pulled himself together, remembering that he had to keep entirely cool. If he allowed the clowns to get under his skin, he would be doing exactly what they wanted. He shook his head. 'Games with clowns!' he said.

Steven reached the end of the ladder and Dodo, watching through the glass booth, saw Joey comically mime his anxiety not to get squished in case Steven fell off the ladder. This time, Dodo did not laugh. The game was no longer funny.

Steven jumped onto the top step, turned around and walked quickly down to the bottom. 'There,' he said.

'Oh dear,' said Dodo, 'Steven's far too big to squeeze through that narrow tube.'

'Well, Joey did,' Clara sniffed.

'Oh, him,' said Dodo contemptuously. 'He's not real anyway, I'm quite sure of that. But what happens if Steven gets stuck half-way through?'

'Then,' said Clara with a smirk, 'we'll simply tie off both ends of the tube and make a large Steven sausage.' Clara began to laugh hysterically at her own joke, but Dodo merely frowned with distaste.

'I don't think that's very funny at all and, come to think of it, I don't think *you're* very funny,' she said,

41

turning her back on the clown.

Steven was trying to get his broad shoulders into the tube. After numerous attempts, he decided to go through on his back.

Relieved to see Steven enter the tube, Dodo rested her brow against the cool glass of the control booth and closed her eyes. Now it seemed that Steven would complete the course and they would succeed in getting the TARDIS back.

When Dodo opened her eyes, she gave a little scream. Down on the floor, Steven's body could be seen wriggling its way through the tube. Above him, Joey stood with a sword upraised as if to cut the tube and Steven in two. He raised the sword. Dodo held her breath. Then, he paused, scratched his nose, brought it down and started eating the blade. The sword was made of silver-coated chocolate.

Dodo smiled in relief. However, the respite was brief. She saw Joey sieze the tube and start to drag it around in a large U, so that it came out at the same place were Steven had entered.

Dodo turned to Clara indignantly. 'Look what he's done,' she said. 'It's not fair.' She pressed the button violently.

But Clara only laughed and clapped her hands like a small child: 'He'll go back to the start line.'

'That's not the way to play games,' said Dodo. 'Let me out of here.' She seized Clara by the front of her costume and shook her. Clara immediately went as limp as a rag doll. 'Open the door at once!'

Clara looked up at her, her head flopping from side to side, laughing. 'I can't.'

'Oh,' said Dodo in exasperation. 'You're just a doll.' She pushed Clara aside and went back to the control panel. 'I shall never laugh at a clown again,' she said.

Meanwhile, Steven finally pulled himself out of the other end of the tube. He straightened up and felt for the home square as he had seen Joey do. Instead, his hands encountered the step ladder. 'Oh no!' Steven exclaimed. He reached up, tore off the blindfold and examined the tube. It had been bent almost entirely back along its length like a horseshoe. Steven realised he had been wasting his time and effort only to come out where he had started. He was livid. He turned on Joey who backed away hastily.

At the same moment, Clara·burst out of the booth, followed by Dodo. 'We've won,' said Clara. 'We've won!' Joey started jumping up and down, making every possible noise with his various bells and horns.

Dodo shouted over their clowns' noise. 'You cheated! Steven completed the course!'

Clara shook her head stubbornly. 'We've won. Now you'll never find your TARDIS.'

'No!' said Steven stubbornly. 'It's a draw. We'll have another round with *him* in the booth this time.' Clara held up Joey's hand. 'The winner!' she cried.

Dodo looked around, picked up Joey's discarded blindfold from the home square and held it up to the light. 'Steven,' she cried, 'look at this. You can see right through it. It's not a real blindfold at all.' They turned round on the clowns who backed away looking somewhat crestfallen.

Steven held up his own blindfold alongside Joey's to compare them, and then turned to the clown. 'No wonder you shot around that course. Now you try it with a real blindfold.' Joey backed away, no longer in a joking mood. Looking as tragic as his face, he began to honk his horn.

Watching them, Dodo suddenly became aware that the Toyroom was becoming darker. The mood was changing from the bright, light hearted clowning to a more sombre, serious note. Joey turned away as if to run, but Steven grabbed his arm.

'Not so fast, laughing boy. Here, Dodo, put the blindfold on him.' As Steven watched Dodo put the blindfold on Joey, Clara stood like a statue, silently watching.

Steven turned to her. 'All right,' he said. 'You'd better go into the booth and guide him.'

Clara, no longer smiling, turned slowly around like an automaton and went into the booth. 'Right,' said Steven. 'Now we'll play the Toymaker's little game, but fairly, this time. Go on. It's your turn.'

Dodo grabbed Joey's hand and led him to the starting point. She waved over to the booth and Clara gave four buzzes. Joey stood, his shoulders hunched, looking old and haggard.

'Go on,' said Steven. Again Clara gave the four buzzes.

Dodo clutched Steven's arm and looked up at him with big anxious eyes. 'Steven, I'm afraid. Have you noticed he's not trying to be funny anymore?'

Steven looked around the room and nodded, as Joey swung across and landed on the first stepping stone, then, carefully, step by step, made his way across them to the foot of the step ladder.

'It seems to be getting darker in here,' said Dodo. 'And' – she shivered slightly – 'there's a draught blowing from somewhere.'

They watched Joey climb up to the top of the steps and set his foot, a little uncertainly, on the first plank. This time he moved stiffly across like an old man, his shoulders hunched, feeling very carefully, a step at a time.

Suddenly the plank began to sway violently. Joey held up his hands in terror as if he was going to fall.

'Steven,' Dodo called. 'You'd better stop him. He'll fall.' She started to move forward but Steven stopped her.

'We can't stop him,' he replied. 'It's us or them, remember.' He shouted across the studio. 'Don't stop now, go on!'

Joey steadied himself and commenced moving across the plank. His steps were getting slower and slower. Inside the booth, Clara started pressing the buzzer again and again.

'She'll throw him off,' said Dodo anxiously. 'Why doesn't she stop that?' Steven shrugged and they both watched, their eyes glued to Joey's every move. The cacophony of buzzing grew louder and louder and the clown began swaying on the plank. 'I can't look,' said Dodo. She covered her eyes with her hands and turned away.

Slowly, Joey toppled sideways and fell down. At the exact same moment, the buzzer started buzzing continuously. As Steven and Dodo looked at the control booth, they saw that Clara had fallen forward and was slumped over the control button,

Abruptly the lights dimmed and went out. At the far end of the room, one of the walls lighted up and there was the TARDIS.

In the Toymaker's private office, the tally recorder was now showing 349. The Doctor's hand hovered for a moment over one of the counters, then made a move. The voice of the Doctor called out with confidence. 'There. I'm only at 350 moves and Dodo and Steven have found the TARDIS, I see.'

'That,' said the Toymaker, standing behind him, 'remains to be seen.'

Steven and Dodo were moving across the room a little cautiously. The room was only illuminated from the area in which the TARDIS stood. 'Is it real?' asked Dodo hesitantly as Steven reached the door.

'She's bright, that one,' commented the Toymaker to the Doctor, as Steven nodded excitedly and pulled the door open. The Doctor leant forward anxiously watching his two companions.

Dodo and Steven rushed forward and inside. 'It's not the TARDIS at all,' said Steven. 'Look!' Inside, there was just the square outline of an empty police phone box.

'What's this?' he said. He bent down and picked up a piece of paper off the floor. Dodo snatched it out of his hand and started reading it.

'It appears to be a riddle,' she said. 'Listen: *Four legs, no feet; of arms no lack; it carries no burden on its back. Six*

46

deadly sisters, seven for choice, call the servants without voice.' She looked at Steven in wonderment. 'What on earth does that mean?'

'It must be a clue of some kind,' said Steven. 'And look, there's a way out at the other end.' The back of the fake TARDIS swung open.

'Perhaps this is to tell us where the real TARDIS is?' Steven shrugged. 'Or perhaps it's just another game. Come on. Either way, we've got to find out.'

He stared to go through, but Dodo hung back, then turned to look at the clowns. All she could see were two small twisted clown figures, now the size of mere dolls. Shocked, Dodo turned and ran quickly after Steven.

4

The Hall of Dolls

'Steven!' Dodo ran up to him breathlessly. 'Those clowns, they've turned into dolls.' But Steven waved his hand at her impatiently then motioned to a large door at the back of the TARDIS.

'I think we'll find the next game beyond this door,' said Steven.

'Are you sure of that?' queried Dodo. Steven nodded and pointed. On the centre of the door was a panel showing the Doctor's tally recorder. The top line read 1023 as before, but the bottom line now read 415.

'That's the Doctor's move recorder for his trilogic game,' said Steven. 'This must be where we go.'

The door was covered by a series of bolts and locks which Steven commenced to undo. Dodo started to help him. 'There,' said Steven as the last bolt was drawn, 'that should do it.' He pushed. 'It won't open.'

'It must,' said Dodo. She threw her body against the door. Then, as the door refused to give, she stepped back impatiently. 'Oh, come on, Steven. It must pull to open. Let's try.'

Both of them took hold of one of the bolts and pulled. The door slowly creaked open. As the door opened, a shaft of rich golden light fell across their faces and they moved forward in wonderment.

They found themselves in a large medieval throne room. Set around the walls were ornate tapestries showing hunting scenes, intermingled with long heraldic banners in rich shades of red, blue and gold. The room was thickly carpeted, and facing them as they entered were four large throne-like chairs. Each chair was different with fine carvings of interweaved flowers and grotesque figures and heads. On each chair was a thick, red, plush cushion. And, strangely, the chairs were numbered one to four.

Meanwhile in the Toymaker's study, the Doctor, with only his hand visible, was continuing the game. His voice sounded satisfied as he gave the familiar dry chuckle. 'Well, well,' he said, 'I haven't made a mistake yet.'

The dark, tall form of the Toymaker materialised beside him. 'Let us hope not, Doctor,' he said. 'I would hate you to end up in my doll's house.' He turned and indicated the Victorian doll's house. 'That is the fate I've reserved for your two friends.'

'Oh, they'll win too,' said the Doctor confidently. 'Don't underrate them. I choose my companions very carefully.'

'Not carefully enough, I'm afraid. They will lose one of the games and end up like the two clowns. We shall be able to amuse ourselves for all of eternity if it suits me. Then, the way I feel, my mood,' the Toymaker extended one of his hands and looked at his long fingernails. 'My mood is going to be very important to you.' He looked up at the scanner. 'Your friends have reached the next test I see. They're in the throne room.'

This obviously started a train of thought in the Doctor's sometimes imperfect memory. 'That game!' he exclaimed. 'I might have known. Steven! Dodo!' he called out. 'Take care! It's chair number –'

Abruptly, the Toymaker reached forward and cut off the interconnecting sound. Then he turned back, his normally self-satisfied expression becoming one of anger. 'You're turning foolish in your old age, Doctor,' he said. 'Now I will be forced to make you dumb as well as invisible. You cannot speak until you reach the second last move of the trilogic game. Now, leave them alone to play their game while you play yours.'

He changed the pitch of his voice slightly to give a direction to the trilogic game. 'Go from move number 442 – and no more tricks if you please.' The Doctor's hand moved towards the board. The Toymaker's face settled down to its usual slightly ironic mocking look and he moved over to his desk. 'Well,' he said thoughtfully, 'your friends managed to outwit my clowns. I shall have to pick some more worthy opponents from now on.'

He pitched up a pack of playing cards and spread them out on the desk. 'I think perhaps the Heart family.' The Toymaker's long fingers probed among the cards and brought out the King, Queen, and Jack of Hearts. 'They've had plenty of experience in a great variety of games.

'And now Doctor,' he said sharply. 'I must have a little chat with your friends.' The Toymaker slowly dematerialised.

*

Dodo and Steven were wandering around the throne room, examining the rich tapestries and banners and the ornate carved chairs that adorned the room. 'You heard the Doctor's voice,' said Dodo. 'I wonder what he was trying to warn us about?'

Steven turned towards the thrones. 'These chairs I imagine,' he said.

As he spoke, the Toymaker materialised in front of him. 'I'm seriously annoyed with your friend,' the Toymaker's tone was sharp and curt. 'Once again he tried to talk to you. For that I had to deprive him of his voice. Let it be a warning to you. Play the games according to the rules or else give up now.'

'The rules, you said,' said Steven. 'Ha!' He laughed scornfully. 'Your players break them. They cheat.'

'Anyway,' Dodo chimed in, 'how can we believe anything you say? Everything here is purely a figment of your imagination.'

Steven nodded. 'For all we know, that voice may not have belonged to the Doctor at all. Perhaps it was you, leading us towards another trap.'

The Toymaker smiled a thin smile. 'I'm glad to see that at last you're treating me with due respect.'

'Only as long as you've got the Doctor!' said Dodo. 'After that, we'll see who the –' The Toymaker abruptly disappeared.

As Steven and Dodo gazed over to where he had been, the door opened and two strangely dressed figures entered: a full-sized live King and Queen of Hearts based upon the playing cards. The Queen was the tallest. She had a proud haughty expression and kept her nose raised as though if she lowered it she would notice some unpleasant odour – the smell of the common people perhaps.

The King on the other hand, was a short, rotund, slightly bewildered-looking monarch with an amiable, almost absent-minded expression on his face. It looked as though he was never quite sure where he was or what he was doing there.

'Is this the room?' said the Queen, her voice high-pitched and imperious. She turned back to the King as he did not respond. 'Is this the room, I said?'

The King blinked and looked around the room. 'I think so, my dear.'

'Then,' said the Queen, looking over at Dodo and Steven with some distaste, 'I suppose these are the people we have to play with.'

'What, my dear?' The King glanced around and then shuffled over and looked Steven and Dodo up and down in a myopic manner. 'I suppose so, my dear. They seem to be a couple of peasants by their dress.'

Dodo looked down at her short skirt. 'I beg your pardon?' she said. 'A couple of peasants?'

'Who are you calling peasants?' cried Steven, but Dodo caught his arm.

'Steven,' she said, 'don't you see who they are?'

'They do look rather familiar,' replied Steven.

'They're playing cards,' said Dodo. 'We are here to play our next game with a couple of playing cards – the King and Queen of Hearts.'

Steven nodded a little glumly. 'The Toymaker's warped sense of humour, I suppose.' The King and Queen, meanwhile, had gone to take a look at the various chairs. Now the Queen turned to the King. 'None of these looks at all like the throne,' she said.

The King, who had once again gone off into some sort of dream world, snapped to. 'Eh?' he said. 'Oh yes my dear. Not like my throne. Oh no, no. They don't, do they? The Toymaker said we'd find them in here though, didn't he?'

Steven turned around to Dodo. 'What's that riddle again?'

'Dodo thought for a minute then replied. *'Four legs, no feet; of arms no lack; it carries no burden on its back.'*

'That must be these chairs then,' said Steven excitedly.

'But what about the rest?' she asked and continued: *'Six deadly sisters, seven for choice,'* she quoted, *'Call the servants without voice.'*

'Oh,' said Steven disappointed. 'It can't be the chairs then; there's only four of them.'

Behind them, the Queen tapped the King on the shoulder with her fan. 'You're not paying the least attention again, Henry. I warned you – if we don't find that throne, the Toymaker will keep us here. We'll be playing cards for all eternity, and thus we shall never rule again.'

The King turned his slightly vacant gaze back towards the Queen. 'Ah,' he said. 'A good point, m'dear. Yes, got to find the throne. This card playing is quite ridiculous; the monarchy is not dead!' He moved over towards the chairs and brought out a monocle which he polished and then proceeded to examine.

Dodo had been watching this exchange with interest. She turned back to Steven. 'What do you make of them?' she queried. 'They seem like real people.'

'I don't make anything of them,' said Steven. 'Let's just ignore them.' He turned away. 'Peasants!' he muttered under his breath. 'They've been sent here to distract us. Look,' he said. 'There's a passage over there. I didn't notice it before. Let's see if there are any further rooms in this palace, or whatever it is.'

After they'd gone, the Queen turned back impatiently to the King. 'Where's that Knave?' she called. 'Cyril! Cyril! Tormenting the Joker as usual, I expect.'

The door was pulled open and a strange-looking couple entered. The first was a lean lugubrious-looking Joker, sad, stoop-shouldered, wearing the Joker's cap and bells and obviously modelled after the playing card of the same name. Behind him, there was a rotund, red-cheeked youth with large, round, innocent-looking blue eyes. He was dressed in the garb of the Jack of Hearts. He was carrying a short sword with which he was prodding the reluctant Joker before him.

The Joker looked over at the King and Queen. His voice was wavery, thin and nasal. 'Did you have to give him that sword?' he asked.

The Queen waved her fan impatiently. 'Quiet, fool! Cyril, what do you think you're doing?'

'Oh, nothing,' said the Jack. 'Just fooling around!' He sheathed his sword. 'I'm hungry.'

The King turned to look at him. 'The boy's always hungry.'

'He's a pig,' the Joker muttered almost inaudibly.

The Queen turned imperiously on him. 'What did you say?'

The Joker waved his cap and bells. 'What's wet, goes down but never up again?' he asked. 'Give up? The rain ... get it?'

'Stop talking nonsense, fool. We must find that throne before those peasants stumble upon it. Where have they gone?' she said, looking around the room.

'Along that passage, my dear,' said the King, who was obviously a little sharper than he appeared.

'Why didn't you tell me before?' said the Queen impatiently. 'We must follow them. Fool,' she snapped, 'you stay here and keep an eye on these chairs. Cyril,' she turned to the Knave, 'stay here with the fool and please stop annoying him!' She swept on into the passage, followed by the King.

Steven and Dodo were standing in another throne room. This room was quite different from the golden one they had just left. It was panelled in a dark oak; wood that looked as though it had been weathered and darkened through the centuries. On the two main facing walls, there were four cupboards: each of them shaped like the TARDIS. In the centre of the room were three more thrones. These were plainer, with less ornate carvings, and without the cushions. They were numbered five, six and seven.

Dodo gave a little start of surprise and pleasure. 'Look Steven,' she said. 'More TARDISes.'

But Steven remained looking at the thrones. 'Three here, and four in there. It *is* the chairs. Don't you see?' he turned back to Dodo. '*Six deadly sisters, seven for choice*. I suppose that means that six of them are dangerous to sit in.

'And only one of them is the right one we have to find to win the game,' said Dodo excitedly.

Steven nodded. 'Yes, it's a deadly kind of musical chairs. Just the sort of game you'd think that evil toymakers would make up. We'll have to work it out by elimination. I wonder how dangerous they are.' Steven walked over to the first chair and was about to lower himself into the seat.

'No!' Dodo screamed. 'Steven don't.'

Steven started up and turned towards her. 'What's the matter now?' he said a trifle crossly.

Dodo pulled him away from the chair. 'Don't risk it. None of the Toymaker's toys are jokes – six of these chairs may destroy us. That may be one of the deadly ones.'

'A charming thought,' Steven nodded ironically. 'You're right, I'm sure.' Steven looked around the room. 'Let's open these cupboards.'

Dodo shuddered. 'They're made to look just like TARDISes. They may be as deadly as the chairs.'

Steven thought for a moment then shook his head. 'I don't think so,' he said. 'Don't forget, the magic number is seven and there are only four of these and there were none in the other room.' He crossed over to the one nearest the door, opened it, then started back in amazement.

'What is it?' cried Dodo, running over to him. She looked inside and gave a little shriek.

Inside the cupboard were two life-size dolls, made up as ballerinas, with large painted eyes, hair, short dance tutus, and ballet shoes.

'It's all right,' said Steven. 'They're only dolls. Let's see if there are any more of these.' He walked over to the second TARDIS cupboard and flung the door open. 'Here look,' he said. Inside were two more of the life-like dolls.

Dodo had by now recovered her equilibrium and nodded. 'That makes four,' she said. 'Let's see what we've got over here.' She ran over to a third TARDIS cupboard and pulled it open. 'Look,' she said. Inside were standing three more dolls: two ballerinas and one male dancer dressed in tights and doublet as though they were ready to dance one of the great classic ballets like *Gisèle* or *Swan Lake*.

'Hey,' said Dodo excitedly. 'This one looks like Rudolph Nureyev.' She was a great ballet fan. She reached in to pull out the male doll but Steven called over and stopped her.

'Don't touch the dolls,' he said.

'What's wrong?' Dodo queried.

'There are seven of them. They could be the deadly ones, or some other dangerous creature. The riddle said *six deadly sisters*. It matches. What was that last line again?'

Dodo tried to remember: 'I've got it. *Call the servants without voice* ... But you can't call something without speaking!'

'Ah,' said Steven. '*They* haven't got voices, that's true, but *we* have, remember, so let's try and see if they obey our commands.' He turned back to one of the cupboards and called out. 'Dolls! Come out!'

Dodo edged slightly behind Steven, waiting to see what would happen, not at all sure she wanted to see these dolls come to life. But nothing happened. The dolls remained where they were, leaning against the walls of the small TARDIS cupboards.

Steven scratched his head. 'They must be the servants,' he said. 'Let's take a risk then.' He reached inside one of the cupboards and pulled a ballerina doll out, then pulled the second one out. He dumped them both on the floor. Next, he moved down to the second cupboard and started bringing out the dolls.

Dodo, meanwhile, was standing there looking at the fourth cupboard. 'With those seven dolls in the three cupboards,' she said. 'I wonder what's in the fourth cupboard.'

'Are you thinking what I'm thinking?' said Steven suddenly looking round. 'Perhaps,' he said, 'it could be the real TARDIS.' He dropped the second pair of dolls on the floor, crossed over to the fourth cupboard, reached out and tried the door.

It wouldn't open.

As Dodo and Steven gazed preoccupied at the fourth cupboard, neither of them noticed the other three doors silently swinging shut behind them.

'It can't be the real TARDIS,' said Dodo disappointed. 'It won't open.'

Steven snapped his fingers. 'But of course,' he said. 'We're being foolish. How can it open? The Doctor has the key.'

'We've forgotten all about him,' said Dodo anxiously. 'I wonder where he's arrived at in the game. I'll check back with the tally recorder, there must be one here somewhere. They're in every other room.' She looked around and spotted the robot, showing the Doctor's

58

tally, standing near the entrance to the room. 'The Doctor's over half-way,' she said. 'Come on, if we're going to use the dolls in the chairs, we'd better hurry before the others get here.'

Dodo and Steven turned to get the dolls only to be confronted by the King and Queen of Hearts who had entered unseen behind them. The Queen nodded meaningfully to the King. 'Those peasants again,' she said. 'What are you doing? Caught you in the act this time.'

The King looked over at the dolls they were carrying. 'They seem to be playing with dolls, m'dear,' he said.

'I can see that,' the Queen said savagely. 'The point is, what are they doing with them?'

Dodo had been studying the King and Queen intently, and she turned to Steven. 'They seem very real to me,' she said. 'I think we ought to talk to them.' She turned to the Queen. 'We're going to use them to test the chairs.'

The Queen's eyebrows rose: 'Test them?'

'Yes,' said Dodo. 'Six are dangerous; only one is safe. You know, I feel very foolish,' she said giggling a little. 'Talking to a playing card.'

The Queen was outraged, her chin went even higher in the air. 'playing card?' she cried.

'Well,' said Dodo, 'aren't you?'

Steven tapped her on the shoulder. 'Listen,' he said. 'It's useless talking to them, they're only the products of the Toymaker's imagination.'

The Queen looked even more indignant. 'We're as real as you are. Henry!' she called.

The King shuffled forward. 'Yes, m'dear?'

'Let this wretched girl feel your arm.'

'Eh what? Feel my arm?' the King said confused.

The Queen impatiently grabbed Dodo's arm and put it onto the King's. 'There child. Isn't that an arm? Not much of one, I grant you – but a real arm nevertheless.'

Dodo looked excitedly over to Steven. 'It is! Steven, these are real people! Feel his arm.'

'I don't want to feel his arm,' Steven said a little pettishly. 'I'll take your word for it.' He turned back to the King and Queen. 'Well, if you're real people, how did you get in here, and how did you get into that ridiculous costume.'

The King nodded a little wearily. 'Oh,' he said. 'It would take too long to explain m'boy, but we're victims of the Toymaker, same as you. Now for instance, if I were to sit in this chair I expect –'

He was about to sit in one of the thrones until the Queen screamed at him. 'Don't sit there! You don't know what will happen!'

'No, of course,' said the King. 'What do we do?'

'We'll have to use the dolls,' said the Queen imperiously. 'Let's each choose a doll and then we can take turns to test out the thrones. Then we'll find out the answer.'

Dodo looked back a little indignantly. 'But that's not fair,' she said. 'We found the dolls, they're ours! We were supposed to be playing against each other.'

'But that can't be right,' said the Queen. 'There are four dolls and four of us. We must be meant to have one each. That's what's fair!'

'Then,' said the King, 'we all have a chance to test a chair before sitting on it ourselves.'

Dodo looked confused for a minute. 'What do you mean one each?' she said. 'What about –' Before she could go any further, Steven quickly cut in. 'It's all right Dodo.'

Dodo still looked confused. 'But what about –' she pointed over to the other cupboards which contained the three dolls.

'I said,' said Steven meaningfully, 'that it'll be all right.'

He edged a little closer to her and said under his breath, '*Belt up.*' Then he turned to the King and Queen. 'Go ahead,' he said. 'Choose your dolls.'

Dodo, still pursuing her line of thought, said, 'I don't understand,' she said to Steven. 'What about the others?'

This time it was the King who cut in. 'Now,' he said, 'don't you fuss yourself, m'dear. The point of this game is to see who picks the chair that isn't dangerous. Whoever does that is the winner. If you win you get your TARDIS back. If we win we get our liberty. All quite simple.'

'They're quite right, Dodo,' said Steven. 'Choose your doll and keep quiet! Come on.'

Dodo nodded. 'Very well.' Steven and Dodo each picked up a doll and set off towards the first throne room. 'Oh, are you going?' said the King, just noticing.

'We'll see you later,' said Steven.

The Queen said, 'I thought we were going to play this together.'

'As there are seven chairs, I thought that Dodo and I might try our luck in the other room. Then we'll all have an equal chance.

'Oh,' said the King. 'Certainly, certainly, anything you like. Good luck.'

Steven, still carrying the doll, walked over to the passageway and called to Dodo, 'Dodo get a move on!'

'All right,' said Dodo a trifle crossly, 'I'm coming. They're rather big for me to handle.' She followed Steven outside.

After they left, the King turned back to the Queen. 'Charming young couple, aren't they.'

The Queen frowned. 'It's not very charming to be told you're not real. I was not amused. Now, which throne.'

'Well,' said the King. 'None of them look much like my throne, m'dear.'

'Then just pick one out at random,' said the Queen.

The King closed his eyes and started: 'Eeny, meeny, miney, mo.' When he got to mo, he was about to put his hand on one of the chairs when the Queen stopped him. 'No, Henry,' she said. 'Put the doll on it – not your hand.'

The King picked the doll up off the floor and threw it on chair number seven. As soon as the doll landed, two clamps came out of the chair – one across the legs, one across the chest, fastening the doll firmly to the chair which then began to vibrate furiously.

'Henry!' cried the Queen appalled. The Hearts looked at the chair. The doll was shaking so rapidly that it seemed that her head would come off.

5

Siege Perilous

Dodo and Steven, preoccupied in dragging their huge life-size ballerina dolls, didn't notice the Joker and Cyril dozing on the thick carpets of the throne room, until Steven fell over them.

'What on earth?' he bagan and then looked down as the Joker squirmed away from him. 'Oh no,' he said. 'Look at this, Dodo. More playing cards!'

Dodo looked down at them and couldn't help smiling at the lugubrious shocked expression of the Joker. 'Look,' she said. 'That one's a Joker and there, there's a Jack.'

Steven picked up the doll, which he had dropped as he tripped, and dragged it over nearer the thrones. He beckoned to Dodo to come over and join him.

When she came up to him, he said in a quick whisper, 'Leave them alone. Concentrate. You nearly gave the game away in the other room. They think there are only *four* dolls. If everyone picks the wrong chair for the dolls, then we are going to need these others. That's why I wanted you to keep quiet about them.'

This outraged Dodo's English sense of fair play. 'Oh, but that's not fair,' she said. 'I mean, they seem so nice and friendly.'

Steven scowled at her. 'That's what you said about

the two clowns and they cheated, didn't they? Can't you remember that we must beat every opponent the Toymaker throws up against us. Otherwise, we'll never get the TARDIS back. This is not a party, you know. This is as dangerous as meeting the Monoids. Only this time, we haven't got space guns to defend us. We've only got our wits.'

'Are you sure,' said Dodo, 'that if we explained that to the King and Queen, they wouldn't help us.'

Steven shook his head: 'It's too great a risk to take. They belong to the Toymaker, always remember that. He wants to keep us here, or at any rate, he wants to keep the Doctor here.'

'I don't understand that,' said Dodo. 'Why does he want to keep the Doctor here?'

'I don't know,' Steven shook his head. 'And it doesn't really matter does it? The important thing is that we must find the TARDIS before he completes all the moves of the game he's playing with the Toymaker. Now,' he said, 'the important thing seems to be to find the lucky chair before the others and sit in it like any other game of musical chairs. Throw your doll,' he said, 'into one of those chairs.'

'Throw it!' exclaimed Dodo. 'It's heavy. I'll just put it there.' She started to lift the doll.

Steven stopped her. 'Look,' he said, 'if you place it in the chair you might get hurt. There might be some form of electric current. I don't want to see either of us electrocuted. Give it to me and I'll throw it on.'

Dodo handed the doll over to Steven who flung it onto the chair marked 'three'. There was a flash which made them start back. Thick black smoke started pouring from the doll.

'Faugh,' exclaimed Steven vainly beating at the clouds of smoke given off by the chair and the doll. The smoke began to clear and they could see the doll, charred, singed and blackened, sprawling grotesquely across the seat.

'Oh no,' said Dodo. 'What happened to her?'

'There,' said Steven. 'As I suspected, some kind of electrocution. That could have been us.'

Dodo nodded grimly. 'I see what you mean by it not being a party.'

Behind them, Cyril the Jack slowly shook himself, overhearing the last sentence. He sat up. 'Party,' he said. 'Is it time for tea yet? I smell crumpets toasting.' He looked over at the burnt doll then wrinkled his nose. 'Or perhaps not crumpets,' he said. 'What's that?' The Jack rose up quickly, looked at Steven and Dodo, and nervously backed away from the chair.

'Don't be scared of us,' said Dodo. She moved towards him but he turned and bolted into the passage to the other throne room.

Steven, meanwhile, had raised the other doll. 'Stand by,' he said. 'It's time we tried out chair number one.' Steven raised his doll and flung it onto the chair.

There was a slow whirring noise and a blade, protruding from the back of the chair, sliced the doll neatly in half which flopped over onto the floor.

Dodo screamed. 'It's horrible,' she said. 'The Toymaker must be mad! Do you really think he wants to kill us?'

Steven indicated the two dolls: 'What do you think?'

'But what do we do now?' asked Dodo.

'We go and get another doll. We've got to get out of this place!' said Steven.

'But we can't go in there,' said Dodo.

'Why?' asked Steven.

'If we go in there and open the cupboard, they'll find out about the three extra dolls!'

Inside the throne room, the now headless doll was still shaking furiously in chair number seven. The Queen turned to the King. 'Henry,' she said, 'Will you turn that thing off?'

The King made a half ineffectual motion towards the throne. 'I don't think I can get near enough, m'dear,' he said. Suddenly the chair stopped shaking and the doll was released, bits and pieces falling onto the floor.

'I wish you'd stop these silly games,' said a voice behind them. They turned to see Cyril.

The King smiled at him. 'There's a nice chair for you over there,' he said. He pointed to number four.

Cyril looked up appalled and shrunk back clutching the Queen's dress. 'Did you hear him, mother?'

'Henry!' said the Queen indignantly.

Cyril sidled round behind her. 'Oh nothing,' said the King. 'A harmless joke, m'dear. Well, let's try the other doll, shall we?'

The King turned, picked up the remaining doll, carried it over to chair number four, hesitated and then flung it on the chair. As they watched, the doll and chair slowly faded away to nothing. 'Well,' said the Queen. 'That leaves us chairs number five and number six. What do you suggest we do now?'

The King thought for a moment. 'Perhaps we'd better see how the young people are making out in their room.'

'They obviously haven't found it yet,' said the Queen. 'We would have had a visit from the Toymaker if they had. He would have been very cross.'

'Yes,' said the King thinking. He tapped his brow. 'You know what we need – we need two more dolls. He looked regretfully at Cyril, now unconcernedly tucking into a banana he had discovered in one of his pockets. Then, turning back to the Queen with a sudden inspiration, he said, 'I know – the fool!'

The Queen looked at him with disdain. 'How can you think of entertainment at a time like this?' Then she followed his gaze to the remaining chair. 'Oh,' she said. 'I see. Of course, the fool!'

The King nodded meaningfully. 'Precisely, m'dear,' he said. He offered his arm to the Queen and they turned to leave for the other room. Cyril stopped eating the banana, glanced back fearfully at the chairs and the broken dolls, then scuttled after them.

Meanwile, Steven was lying partly under chair number two. As Dodo watched, he put a tentative hand up towards it. 'No!' she screamed at him. 'Steven, be careful!'

Steven crawled out from under. 'You can't tell anything by looking at it,' he said. 'We'll just have to get those other two dolls.'

'Shush,' said Dodo, 'the King and Queen are coming.'

Steven nodded. 'Good. I'll try to distract them. I'll hold them here while you slip along to the other room and try the other chair. That will eliminate that room completely and then it will be one of these two chairs.'

The King and Queen entered. 'Ah,' said the King breezily. 'We've been having a great time trying out our thrones.'

'Yes,' said the Queen to Dodo. 'Why don't you try one of those chairs, child?'

Dodo put her tongue out at her. 'Why don't you?'

'Oh,' the Queen exclaimed and turned her back on Dodo.

Steven turned to the King. 'So you've had no luck either? Well, if you're out of dolls too,' Steven winked quickly at Dodo who turned and ran down the passage between the two rooms, 'it looks rather like stalemate.'

'Ah, not quite, m'boy', said the King. 'We still have another card to play.' He laughed slightly. 'If you'll pardon the expression.' The King turned and looked down at the sleeping Joker, then stirred him with his foot.

The Joker stirred sleepily and slowly clambered up to his feet. 'What's black and white and read all over?' he said.

Steven looked puzzled for a moment. 'I don't know,' he said. 'A newspaper,' said the Joker.

'Oh, I didn't wake you up for a joke, m'boy,' said the King. 'Anyway, I've heard all your riddles before. No, we just want your advice this time, don't we m'dear?' he said to the Queen.

The Queen looked her most haughty. 'What!' she said. 'Advice from a fool?'

The King cocked his eyebrow at her. 'To pick our new throne, m'dear. Eh, what?' he said. 'Now, for instance' – he turned to the Joker – 'what would you say to this fine throne here?' The King took the Joker's arm and led him over to chair number two. Steven grasped what the King was after and ran forward, blocking their way to the throne.

'Uh, uh,' Steven said. 'Not in this chair.' The Joker looked confusedly from the King to Steven wondering what the fuss was about, when Dodo ran into the room. 'Steven,' she said. 'The cupboard with the other three dolls, it's locked! I can't open it.'

Steven turned back. 'You must be able to, it was open before.'

The Queen turned, outraged. 'What?' she said. 'Three more dolls?'

The King raised his finger and waggled it. 'And you were keeping them from us? Naughty.'

'Cheats,' said the Queen in her deepest voice.

'*You* can talk,' said Steven. 'After what you were about to do to that poor fellow.' Steven pointed to the Joker.

'Eh?' said the Joker. 'What's that?'

'Nothing, my dear old chap,' said the King, calming him. 'Come with us. We won't leave you in such company.'

'No, certainly not,' said the Queen. 'I abhor cheats. Come, Cyril.' The King and Queen swept out of the room. Cyril put his tongue out at Steven and Dodo and ran after them. The Joker hesitated, lost in some train of thought and walked after them muttering, 'Poor fellow? Poor fellow?' to himself.

As soon as the Hearts had left the room, Steven turned angrily back to Dodo. 'Now you've done it. Handed the game to them on a platter. If the right chair is not in this room, we've lost the game.'

Dodo folded her arms obstinately. 'I don't see that,' she said. 'Anyway, we'll win fairly.'

'Look,' said Steven explaining. 'They have two chairs left, right? They'll get the Joker to sit on one. If that's not the right chair, then the other must be the winner.' Steven gave Dodo a long look of disgust, then turned away from her and crossed his arms.

Feeling guilty, Dodo ran up to him, but he just turned away. Almost in tears at having ruined their chances, Dodo turned back towards the chairs. Then, coming to a sudden resolution, she walked over to chair number two and started to lower herself upon it.

In the Toymaker's study, the Toymaker was leaning back watching the hand of the Doctor playing the trilogic game. 'You see,' he said. 'It's quite easy when you try and don't let yourself be distracted by your friends. You've been moving along quite satisfactorily.' The Toymaker pointed over at the tally register. It now recorded 690 moves. 'It's especially commendable since Dodo has chosen to sit in the wrong chair.'

The Doctor's hand paused and remained stiffly in the air as if the owner was looking over at the screen.

'Yes,' said the Toymaker. 'The freezing chair.'

Back in the throne room, Dodo, sitting on throne number two, let out a shriek. Steven whipped around. 'Dodo, what are you doing?' he said. Steven rushed across to her only to be met by some kind of invisible wall set around the throne.

'Steven,' said Dodo, her teeth chattering. 'I'm cold all the way through.'

'Stand up,' said Steven urgently. 'I can't get through to you. There's some sort of barrier here.'

'Help me,' said Dodo plaintively. 'I'm freezing. I can't move.'

'Stand up,' said Steven.

Dodo shook her head. 'I can't! I can't!'

'You must,' said Steven. 'There's some kind of wall around you. You must try.'

'I think I'm turning to ice, Steven,' she said.

'Fight the cold, fight it! You must get out of that chair. Fight it, Dodo. Now! Together – One –' Steven extended his hand. This time the barrier seemed to part as their combined wills dissipated it. Steven's hand gripped Dodo's. Immediately he felt an intense cold penetrating his hand and arm.

Dodo shook her head. 'It's no use, Steven. It will freeze you as well. Let go!'

'No,' said Steven. 'We must meet it together. Quick now – one pull!'

For one moment it seemed as though the Toymaker's deadly chair was going to win. Then, as Steven and Dodo exerted their last ounce of will and determination, they countered the influence of the chair. With one great rush, Dodo was ripped out of the chair and fell on top of Steven as they tumbled over together.

'Oh,' said Dodo, 'thank you.' Her teeth were chattering. 'Thank you, you did it.'

Steven, gasping for breath and rubbing his frozen hand, shook his head. 'No, Dodo. We did it together. It was our combined wills. It shows what can happen if we act together. We can beat this wicked man.'

'But, Steven,' said Dodo, rubbing back the circulation into her body, 'we've lost, don't you see? They've probably found the lucky chair by now and with it, the TARDIS.'

6

The Last Deadly Sister

The King and Queen were standing by chairs five and six with the Joker. Behind them, Cyril was squatting on the ground eating another banana.

The King turned to the Joker. 'Now, my good fellow,' he said, 'we would be very glad of your honest opinion. Which of these two is the better throne for me.'

The Joker gazed from the King to the Queen a little suspiciously. He hadn't forgotten the remark about his being a poor fellow. Then he looked over at the chairs. 'Well,' he said, 'That one isn't too bad.' He pointed to number six.

The King looked over at it and inspected it through his monocle. 'Number six, eh? Good, good, but there's only one way to really test a chair, isn't there? You can't tell much by just looking.'

The Joker looked suspiciously over at the pieces of broken doll on chair number one. 'Poor fellow,' he muttered to himself. 'What did he mean?'

'Come on, Fool,' said the Queen impatiently. 'We haven't got all day.'

The Joker tried to manage a smile and waved his jester's wand. 'Wouldn't you rather have a riddle?' he said. 'When is a door not a door?'

'Eh?' said the King and then laughed. 'He's got us

there, m'dear.'

'Everyone knows that!' chimed in Cyril, his mouth full of banana. 'When it's ajar.'

'Faugh! That's not even funny,' said the Queen. 'Are you going to sit in the chair or not?' She was becoming more and more impatient with the Joker.

'Oh, all right,' agreed the Joker. He shuffled unwillingly over to the chair and began to lower himself. Just then, Cyril gave a stifled giggle.

The Joker raised himself again and looked over suspiciously. 'What's he laughing at?' he said.

The Queen turned warningly to Cyril. 'You're not laughing, are you?'

Cyril, still coping with a mouthful of banana, shook his head and then spluttered, unable to contain his guffaw.

The Joker wearily raised his eyes. 'And they call me a fool,' he said.

'Come now,' said the King. 'Sit down, my dear fellow.'

But the Joker had had enough and moved away. 'Not on your life, sire,' he said. He backed away to the passage. 'A joke is a joke, but this is too much. I'm giving notice, you'll have to try out your own chairs.' He raised his jester's wand in a final slightly rude gesture, and left.

After he had gone, the King and Queen looked after him astonished. Then the King turned around to Cyril and raised his hand. Cyril scrambled to his feet. 'After him,' said the King. Cyril scurried out the door and the King turned back to the Queen: 'Your son, m'dear.'

'More yours,' said the Queen. 'Anyway, what do we

do now?'

'Nothing else for it,' said the King. 'You'll have to try, m'dear.'

The Queen drew herself up to her full height and looked at him majestically. '*I*?' she said.

'Oh,' said the King a little hastily, 'one of us, I mean. We'll have to draw matches.' He brought out a box of matches and opened it up. 'Whoever gets the short match sits in the chair,' he said.

The Queen shook her head firmly. 'I don't trust your matches,' she said. She felt in the pocket of her gown and brought out a coin. 'We'll have to toss for it.' She spun it up in the air. 'Heads,' she said.

The King nodded and waggled his finger. 'You forget, m'dear. I know that coin – it's got two heads.'

The Queen shrugged her shoulders impatiently and put the coin away. 'Then, she said, 'we'll both sit on the chair together. So if we go ...'

'We go together, my love,' said the King.

In the first touch of real feeling displayed by the couple, the King offered the Queen his arm. They walked over to chair number six and slowly sat down.

Almost at once, the chair collapsed entangling and imprisoning the King and Queen in the wreckage, just as Steven and Dodo entered.

'Oh, the poor things,' said Dodo. 'Quick, Steven we must get them out of there.'

'Right,' said Steven. 'But not just now.' He pointed over at chair number five. 'Look,' he said.

Dodo caught on quickly. 'You mean?'

'That must be the one,' said Steven. He walked over to it and without hesitating, sat down. The room darkened and a light came on from the cupboard that wouldn't open. It now began to slide out as they watched until finally it stood almost clear of the wall – an unmistakable police box. But was it the real TARDIS?

'We've won!' exclaimed Dodo. 'That's got to be the TARDIS! As soon as the Doctor wins his game, we can go. Oh, thank goodness Steven, we're safe, we've won!'

She ran over to the TARDIS, took the handle and opened the door. Inside, as Steven came to join her, they saw the interior of a perfectly ordinary police telephone box. 'Oh no,' she said. 'It can't be, it's got to be the real one. Don't say it's happened again.'

'This must be another of the Toymaker's TARDISes,' said Steven. He stepped inside and started searching through it. 'Nothing,' he said. 'Absolutely nothing. What now?'

'You know,' said Dodo, 'we didn't really sort out the last riddle about calling the servants without voice.'

Steven nodded glumly. Both of them were deeply disappointed by the way things had turned out after all their efforts. 'Let's try it again,' said Steven. 'You never know.' He walked out of the box. 'Dolls, dolls wherever you are, come out.'

Suddenly behind him, came the ring of the telephone. The phone in the police box was ringing. Steven turned and answered it while Dodo gazed fearfully at the cupboard with the three dolls. But nothing seemed to be happening. Steven picked up the phone a little tentatively and put it to his ear. The unmistakable low drawling tones of the Toymaker came over the ear piece.

'You're doing better than I thought,' he said. 'But don't rest on your laurels. The Doctor's succeeding even faster than you. Time and luck are running out. Anyway,' he said, 'Here is the next clue:

> Hunt the key to fit the door
> That leads out on the dancing floor;
> Then escape the rhythmic beat,
> Or you'll forever tap your feet.'

There was a click and then a dial tone.

Steven turned around to Dodo. 'He's gone,' he said. He put the receiver back and as he did so, the entire back wall of the police box swung open to reveal a darkened passage. Steven turned back to Dodo. 'Look, Dodo,' he said, 'this is obviously where the next game is.'

Dodo nodded and then turned back to look at the chairs. 'We still have to release the King and Queen before we go. I rather liked them, Steven. They were human in their own way.' She turned and walked back over towards the throne, then stood still in sudden shock. Steven joined her. They looked at the throne. Lying on the seat were two playing cards – the King and Queen of Hearts.

Steven turned back to Dodo and shrugged. 'I said that's all they were,' he said. 'On to the next game. Come on.'

Dodo hung back for a moment, as Steven entered the passage. 'Let's try the dolls once more,' she said. She then called out, 'Dolls, dolls wherever you are, come out.' She paused for a moment and glanced around the room but again, nothing happened. Steven called impatiently down the passageway and she hurried after him.

As soon as the two of them made off down the passage, the lights began to come on again in the room.

All four covered doors slid open and the three dolls started moving, slowly and jerkily out of their cupboard and across the floor to the police box.

7

Enter Mrs Wiggs and Sergeant Rugg

The Toymaker stood facing the silent, invisible Doctor. 'I must congratulate you on your choice of friends, Doctor. A very astute couple. Neither of my teams has been able to beat them so far. They've earned a little amusement, I think.'

The Toymaker turned back to one of the doll's houses – the Victorian one. 'Now who have we here that will amuse them,' he said. 'Upstairs?' He wondered, looking at the top rooms of the house. 'No, I think we shall find more worthy opponents downstairs ... Perhaps in the kitchen.'

Steven and Dodo were now at the end of the long darkened passageway which led from the second throne room. Steven was throwing his weight against the large door that stood at the end. The door was Victorian, made of heavy mahogany and panelled. Steven stood back and rubbed his bruised shoulder. 'It's no use,' he said. 'I can't seem to get it open.'

'Oh, my goodness,' said Dodo behind him. 'Look there – the servants!' As Steven turned around, he saw, advancing towards him with their slow stiff gait, the three dolls.

'The servants without voice,' Dodo continued. 'They've come to our call.'

Dodo, frightened, pressed back against Steven. 'They scare me,' she said.

Steven's voice was a trifle nervous. 'They're only dolls.'

'We called them,' said Dodo. 'Perhaps we can make them go back to their cupboard.' She called out as the dolls continued their slow inexorable advance towards them. 'Dolls,' she said, 'go back! Go back to your cupboard!'

The dolls still continued to stalk down the corridor towards them.

Steven moved forward. 'I'll stop them,' he said squaring his powerful shoulders. But Dodo grasped his arm.

'Don't, Steven,' said Dodo. 'You don't know what they might do. After all, we helped destroy their companions, the other dolls.'

'Then perhaps we can edge past them,' said Steven.

As if reading his mind, the three dolls spread out and stopped, completely blocking the passageway.

'We can't get past them now,' said Dodo anxiously.

'But they've stopped,' said Steven. 'I'm going to rush them, knock them over. You follow me. We'll get past them.' Steven hunched his shoulders and moved back to get a good run at the dolls. As he moved back, the solid kitchen door swung silently open behind him and he backed into it without noticing.

'Be careful, Steven,' cried Dodo. She turned around and noticed the open door. 'Look!' She grasped his arm, throwing him slightly off balance.

Steven fell back against the wall. 'What did you do that for?' He turned and saw the open door. 'Oh, good heavens,' he said.

Dodo moved forward into the kitchen, Steven cautiously following her. 'Careful,' he warned. 'It could be a trap.'

The kitchen they moved into was an exact replica of the Toymaker's doll kitchen with a large Welsh dresser housing gleaming Willow pattern cups and plates, and a long deal topped table complete with mixing bowls, rolling pin and pastry board.

On one side, was a long deep ceramic sink with a wooden draining board; on the other, a large coal burning range with oven and hobs on which a variety of saucepans were simmering.

'A trap.' The voice came from behind them, deep, mellow and fruity. 'A trap, in here, in Mrs Wiggs' kitchen! You'll have to watch your language, young fellow.'

Steven and Dodo wheeled around to see standing by the table, a red-faced, mustachioed, somewhat portly middle-aged man, smartly dressed in a red uniform with white breaches and crossed belts over his chest which Steven, who studied and liked reading books about military history, was quick to recognise as a sergeant's uniform from the time of the Napoleonic Wars.

'Yes,' said another voice. They turned to find a comfortably plump, middle-aged woman with a mop cap perched on her head, and a red mottled face, the result of standing over too many hot stoves. She spoke with a cockney accent. 'What do you want in my kitchen?' she asked.

Dodo, pleased to see somebody who looked almost normal – after the clowns and the playing cards, stepped forward. 'We're looking for the next game. Perhaps you can help us? The clue goes:

> Hunt the key to fit the door,
> That leads out on the dancing floor;
> Then escape the rhythmic beat,
> Or you'll forever tap your feet.'

'Well,' said Mrs Wiggs (for that was her name), 'only dancing floor I knows of is through there.' She pointed off at the other end of the kitchen where there was an old oak door with a large lock and keyhole.

'Oh, thank you,' said Dodo. She started walking across to the door while Steven stayed behind, looking curiously around the kitchen.

The Sergeant drew himself up to his full height. 'Right then, young fella m'lad. No loitering. Pick your feet up. Hup two, three, four; hup two, three, four.'

Steven turned around to him contemptuously. 'You look like a toy soldier to me. Why don't you go back to your box?'

'What's that?' the Sergeant raised his hand and twisted one of his long moustaches. 'You young whipper snapper! I'll, I'll –'

Steven turned on him again. 'You'll what?' he said.

'Well,' said the Sergeant, backing away. 'I'll uh – You need a good hiding, m'lad!'

After all he'd been through, Steven was spoiling for a fight. 'Who's going to give it to me?' he said. The Sergeant backed away again and Mrs Wiggs came forward.

'No fisticuffs in my nice clean kitchen, Sergeant,' she warned.

The Sergeant nodded. 'Just as well you spoke, Cook.

82

No telling what I might have done to him if you hadn't stopped me.'

Mrs Wiggs looked at him fondly. 'You're a terrible man when you're roused, Sergeant.'

The Sergeant twirled his moustache again; his eyes were twinkling. 'Army training, Cook. Six years with the Iron Duke.'

Dodo had been trying the door handle without success, then she turned back. 'The door seems to be locked. But I'm sure we must get through here. That's what the clue says. The TARDIS must be out on the dance floor.'

Steven came over, tried the door, then kicked it. 'How can the Toymaker expect us to play his crazy games if he locks all his doors!'

The Sergeant lowered his voice and nudged Mrs Wiggs. 'Like to have him in my mob,' he said. 'Just give me a week. I'll make a man of him.'

'What?' Steven turned back threateningly.

'Uh,' said the Sergeant. 'Well, like, not that he needs making a man of. I'm sure he's that already – but just to sharpen him up a bit, like.'

'Now,' said Steven, 'I'm warning you.' He moved towards the Sergeant.

Dodo came forward and took his arm, smiling at him. 'Really, Steven,' she said laughing, 'if they're not real, how can you lose your temper with them?'

Steven looked puzzled and scratched his head. 'You can't have it both ways, you know,' said Dodo.

'All right,' said Steven. 'We'll just ignore them. They're obviously sent to get my goat. Well, where do we go from here? We're stuck.'

The Sergeant came over to Dodo and looked her over. 'The Iron Duke wouldn't have been stuck over a little thing like that,' he said.

Steven gritted his teeth and turned to Dodo. 'Okay, Dodo, it's your turn.'

Dodo turned round and smiled at the Sergeant. 'What would the Iron Duke have done?' she said.

The Sergeant smiled a little enigmatically. 'Have had another look at the riddle, I expect,' he said.

'The riddle ...' said Dodo. She thought for a moment. '*Then escape the rhythmic beat, or you'll forever tap your feet.*'

'Naw,' said Mrs Wiggs. 'The first bits, ducks.'

'*Hunt the key to fit the door* – Steven,' she said, 'that's it!'

Steven looked blank for a moment. 'Don't you see?' said Dodo. 'The game is Hunt The Thimble. Only instead of a thimble, it must be a door key. She looked over at the door. 'And a rather large one at that.'

'Hmm,' Steven nodded slowly in agreement. 'I see,' he said. 'The problem is, where do we start looking?' They glanced around the large over-furnished Victorian kitchen with its pots, pans, canisters, shelves and dishes.

Dodo walked over to the range and then gave a start as she noticed something she hadn't seen before. In a large chair, to the right of the range, was a sleeping kitchen boy, dressed in a chef's hat, rather grubby white coat and trousers.

'Steven,' she said, 'look at this fellow.'

'That's my kitchen boy,' said Mrs Wiggs, 'Lazy good-for-nothing. He spends all his time sleeping and eating.'

'But don't you think,' said Dodo to Steven, 'that he looks rather like Cyril?'

Steven glanced down at the sleeping boy and nodded. 'Come to think of it he does. But then, all the Toymaker's creations look alike to me. We'd better get a move on,' he said.

He looked up over the door to where the inevitable robot now stood. 'Look,' he said. On the screen the number read 813. 'We must find the TARDIS before the Doctor reaches 1023. We haven't long,' said Steven. He turned to the range and lifted up one of the saucepans. The lid was hot; he dropped it with a cry. 'Ow!' he said.

'Comes from a 'ot place, don't it?' said Mrs Wiggs. 'What do you expect? Now come away from me pans.'

'We've got to find the key to that door,' said Dodo.

'You won't find it there,' said Mrs Wiggs.

'How do you know?' said Dodo.

The Sergeant stepped forward once more to defend the cook: ''Cause, Mrs Wiggs always knows what's best. That's why, young lady.'

Steven had a sudden idea, went over to the sleeping boy and started lifting him up to see if the key was perhaps underneath where he was lying. Despite the boy's weight, Steven managed to lift him clear of the chair and looked. There was no key there. He put him back.

Dodo took one more look around the kitchen, and decided on another tack. She turned to the Sergeant, went up to him and smiled her most beguiling smile. 'You'll help us find the key,' she said. 'Won't you?'

'Hmm,' the Sergeant twirled his moustache. 'Well, I

dunno.'

'Oh,' said Dodo. 'You look so marvellous in that uniform. You must be very brave.'

'Well, I do my duty, gel.'

'Then you'll help us,' said Dodo. 'For my sake.' She put her hand on the Sergeant's chest and opened her eyes wide.

The Sergeant gazed down at her. Soldiers could never resist the fair sex, as he would have put it. 'All right, gel,' he said. 'For you mind.' He stuck his thumb over his shoulder at Steven. 'Not for 'im.'

Dodo nodded eagerly. 'Where do you suggest we start looking?'

'Hm,' said the Sergeant. 'Let's see. How 'bout the old dresser here?'

Meanwhile Mrs Wiggs was busy at the table making pastry and keeping an eye on this exchange with growing disfavour. 'You watch what you do with my dresser,' she said a little jealously.

Disregarding her, Dodo opened a drawer and started rummaging around the knives and forks inside. The Sergeant opened another and started throwing table-cloths and cloth napkins out on the floor.

Steven, meanwhile, took a chair over, stood on it and started examining the inside of a large cuckoo clock, just as it struck. The cuckoo came out and narrowly missed hitting him on the nose. Steven fell back off the chair.

'Are you all right?' called Dodo. Then as Steven started getting to his feet, Dodo couldn't resist laughing, as she always did at Steven's mishaps. He always looked so comically protective of his dignity.

''ere, what do you thinks this place is, a bloomin'

fairground?' Mrs Wiggs was outraged as she saw Sergeant Rugg empty out another drawer of linen. 'You put all of that back in the drawer, just as it was!'

The Sergeant turned back and stood to attention. 'Just 'elping the young lady, Mrs Wiggs.' He turned back to Dodo. 'What's your name m'gel?'

Dodo flashed him a smile. 'Dodo,' she said. 'Dodo,' said the Sergeant. 'What a lovely name. Dodo. I like that, I do.'

'Well,' said Mrs Wiggs crossly, 'go and like it somewhere else and take your friends with you.'

The Sergeant turned back towards the cook a little patronisingly. 'Come now, Mrs Wiggs. The young gel's gone and been and lost her key, ain't she?'

'Well,' said Mrs Wiggs, 'she won't find it 'ere.' She grabbed the rolling pin and started rolling up her sleeves.

Steven looked at Dodo and shrugged. 'Take no notice of it, Dodo. She's sent by the Toymaker to put us off. It's a sign we're getting warm.'

He started to crawl under the table to see if the key was there. Getting angry and more red in the face than ever, Mrs Wigg looked from Steven to Dodo, but as neither of them seemed to be taking the slightest notice of her, she put down her roller and went back to her pastry board and started preparing a pie for the oven.

Dodo walked over to one of the cupboards on the dresser and looked inside. She saw a collection of Victorian china: a cow creamer, a swan-shaped butter dish, a china cheese cover made in the shape of a cottage and a stack of dessert plates with Victorian nursery rhymes painted on the rims. She started to search among the china for the key.

By the table Mrs Wiggs suddenly gave a little scream, drew back and looked under. 'Ey,' she said to Steven, 'that was my foot you got hold of. Come out from under there!'

Steven crawled out from under the table. He looked over at Dodo and shook his head. 'It's not under there,' he said. 'Any luck?'

Dodo finished examining the china, turned back and closed the cupboard. 'No,' she said. 'I'll look among the plates up there,' she said, nodding up to the shelves at the top of the dresser. She turned and started dragging her chair over.

'Now don't you get up there, m'gel,' said the Sergeant. 'You'll fall down and break a leg. Here, let me look for you.'

Dodo, touched by this unexpected courtesy and warming to being treated like a woman at last, said, 'It's very kind of you.'

The Sergeant climbed up on the chair. 'Not at all, ma'am,' he said. He wavered for a moment and nearly fell.

Mrs Wiggs glared up at him. 'What do you think you're doing up there, Sergeant.?'

'Now,' said the Sergeant. 'Don't you fret, cookie,' he said. He swayed alarmingly and grabbed the shelf for balance. 'I'll be all right.'

'I'm not worried about *you*,' said Mrs Wiggs. 'It's my china.' As she spoke, the Sergeant pulled a plate out to look behind it. It fell down to the floor and broke. Mrs Wiggs gave a little scream. 'Me best plates! Come down at once!'

'Only a little accident, Mrs Wiggs,' said the Sergeant with dignity.

Mrs Wiggs put her hands on her hips and glared up at him. 'Accident!' she said. 'That was no accident, Sergeant. You threw that plate down deliberate like!'

The Sergeant's face grew solemn. 'I hope as you're not calling me a liar, Mrs Wiggs!' Another plate came crashing down on the floor.

'That,' said Mrs Wiggs ironically, 'was another accident, I suppose.'

The Sergeant changed hands and a few more plates came down. Dodo looked from one to the other, nervous at having started a fight between them. 'Perhaps you'd better come down. Sergeant?' she suggested.

'Not at all, gel, I'm perfectly all right.' Three more plates cascaded down. The kitchen boy began to stir.

'I'm warnin' you, Sergeant Rugg, come down here this instant!' ordered Mrs Wiggs.

The Sergeant's back became ever more ram-rod straight. 'Soldiers don't take orders from civilians, Cook. Now you just pipe down.'

This was the final straw as far as Mrs Wiggs was concerned. 'Pipe down yourself, you great lump!' she said furiously. 'Call yourself a soldier! You'd run away from a pussy cat!'

The Sergeant glared back at her. 'You didn't ought to have said that, Cook.' He deliberately scooped off three more plates, one of them hitting the kitchen boy on the head as it fell. Coming awake with a start, the boy dived below the table.

'You clumsy brute,' said Mrs Wiggs.

'Please, please,' said Dodo very distressed by what

was going on. 'Stop, it's all my fault.'

Steven turned back from examining the big copper boiler in the corner. 'Ignore them,' he said. 'It's being done to prevent us from finding the key. They don't exist, remember – it's not real.' Just then, a plate flung by the Sergeant hit him on the head. 'Oww!' he called.

Dodo pulled him back out of the firing line. 'Are you sure about that?' she questioned.

Steven rubbed his head. 'That certainly felt real enough,' he said. 'Do you suppose there is a key? We've looked everywhere, haven't we? We looked around the kitchen.'

By now a fusilade of missiles was flying back and forth across the kitchen, with Mrs Wiggs picking up the pastry she had been working on and flinging it at the Sergeant who, in turn, was bombarding her with plates. The once orderly kitchen was now a mess of broken crockery, flour and pastry.

Taking advantage of the cook's distraction, the kitchen boy reached up and grabbed a jar of sultanas and then starting eating under the table.

'Oh please, stop, stop!' cried Dodo. 'You've thrown everything there is to throw. Can't you both call a truce?'

'Not everything!' Mrs Wiggs picked up a bag of flour and threw it. It burst like a bomb on the Sergeant's shoulder covering him with white powder. 'He's broken all of me best china!' said Mrs Wiggs.

'I'm sure he'll apologise,' said Dodo.

The Sergeant shook his head and started brushing the flour off. 'Soldiers never apologise,' he said.

Dodo went over to him and, taking a whisk, began to

help him brush the white flour from his red uniform. 'But a gentleman would always apologise to a lady,' she said.

'Garn,' came the voice of Mrs Wiggs behind them. 'Who told ya soldiers were gentlemen?'

'Sergeant Rugg is,' said Dodo. 'I'm sure of that.'

The Sergeant stiffened again, and after a pause turned around and bowed to the cook as she climbed off her chair. 'I apologise,' he said.

Dodo turned back to Mrs Wiggs. 'Now will you accept his apology?'

Mrs Wiggs scowled sulkily for a moment and then said, 'Well, all right, but he'll have to pay for me china.'

'Hmm?' the Sergeant reddened again. 'Pay for the china?' He turned to Dodo. 'You see now why soldiers never apologise? Give the old trout an inch and –'

'*Old trout!*' Mrs Wiggs picked up a broom beside the stove and started after the Sergeant who backed away around the table.

'Now Mrs Wiggs,' he said, 'put that down!'

Mrs Wiggs swept the broom at his legs and as he jumped back, Cyril got it on the head. Crawling out from under the kitchen table still clutching the sultanas, Cyril made for the far wall and crept along it heading for the safety of the walk-in pantry.

Steven followed him with his eyes. 'Hey!' he called to him. 'Just a minute, where do you think you're going.'

The kitchen boy put his tongue out. 'Mind your own business,' he said.

With sudden intuition, Steven strode across to him. 'I think you know where the key is.' Behind them, the cook had the Sergeant bottled in the corner of the room and was belabouring him with the broom despite Dodo's efforts to stop her.

The kitchen boy slowly extended the jar of sultanas towards Steven who took them. 'Now we're getting somewhere.' He put his hand in the jar, feeling around through the sultanas, but there was no key. He tried again – same result. Finally, he dumped them on the floor in disgust.

Meanwhile, the kitchen boy had reached the safety of the pantry. As Steven turned back to him, he slipped inside and shut the door. 'Hey, come out of there.' Steven ran to the door of the pantry and shook it, but the boy had managed to lock himself inside.

'Please don't,' Dodo said to the cook. 'I'm sure you'll hurt him with that broom.'

The Sergeant moved around to the other side of the table out of range and picked up the pie Mrs Wiggs was preparing for the cupboard. 'If she does, this pie gets hurt as well,' he threatened.

'Put me pie down!' said Mrs Wiggs demandingly.

'Put that broom down then!' cried the Sergeant. Mrs Wiggs made a sudden dash around the table, sweeping the broom at the Sergeant's legs. He jumped up on one of the kitchen chairs, holding the pie high above his head.

With a sudden flash of intuition, Dodo turned and clutched Steven's arm. 'Steven,' she said. 'That's the only place we haven't looked!'

'Where?' said Steven.

'The pie,' said Dodo.

'I see what you mean.' Steven picked up the second broom and went to the other end of the table.

He turned to Mrs Wiggs. 'I'll help you,' he said. 'I'll swipe him from behind.'

The Sergeant turned around in alarm, looking at this new enemy that appeared. 'Not you too!' he said.

As Mrs Wiggs swung her broom at him from the front, the Sergeant jumped back and Steven, swinging from the rear, knocked the pie out of his hands. It landed on the floor beside Dodo.

Dodo quickly picked the pie up and ripped the crust off. There inside was a large Victorian key. She showed it to Steven.

'I've got it! This must be the key.'

Steven ran over and grabbed it from her. 'Right,' he said. 'Quick, Dodo.' He ran to the door followed by Dodo and thrust the key in the lock. The door creaked open and as it did so, they could hear the sound of waltz music.

Dodo turned around. 'Thank you, Sergeant,' she said. 'You really are a true gentleman.' She turned to Mrs Wiggs. 'And sorry about your kitchen,' she said.

With the finding of the key, the Sergeant and Mrs Wiggs had stopped fighting and stood looking at them.

Steven and Dodo disappeared. In their place there slowly materialised the tall dark form of the Toymaker.

He turned around to the Sergeant and the Cook who cowered away from him. 'Wretched pair,' he said. 'I give you a chance for freedom and this is all you can do with it. Look at the kitchen.'

The Sergeant came to attention and saluted. 'It's my fault,' said the Sergeant gallantly. 'Not hers.'

The Toymaker sneered at him. 'Such gallantry,' he said. 'From a mere doll! And listen to me both of you.

Tidy yourselves up and get out on that dance floor. At the far end is the TARDIS. Steven and Dodo must be prevented from getting to it at all costs. Do you understand? Fail me and I'll break you like these plates.' The Toymaker turned, lifted the remaining plate off the dresser and smashed it on the table.

Frightened, the Sergeant and the cook nodded and started brushing their clothes, preparing for the dance.

8

The Ballroom

Steven and Dodo stepped out into a room that was in complete contrast to the two previous ones. This room was decorated as an old-fashioned ballroom. A huge chandelier slowly turned, flashing vari-coloured lights across a triangular dance floor of beautifully polished parquet wood. The music was gentle and soothing: old time waltzes, quick steps and fox trots. On the dance floor, three ballerina dolls, one male and two females, were doing a slow graceful dance number. Dodo and Steven stopped to watch.

The dance ended, the dolls took their bows to Dodo's applause, and then relapsed stiffly to a mannequin-like position. Steven, who had been watching the dancing a little impatiently, moved forward to step on the wooden dance floor but Dodo stopped him.

'Be careful,' she said. 'It may be dangerous – like the chairs.'

'There's no other way to get to the TARDIS,' said Steven.

Dodo shook her head. 'Remember what we've been through. It can't be that simple, can it? There must be a catch to it somewhere.' She went on to quote the riddle. '*Then escape the rhythmic beat, or you'll forever tap your feet.* What do you suppose that means?' For answer

Steven cautiously stretched his hand over the dance floor. A slow waltz started up. He pulled his hand back. The music stopped.

'Strange,' said Dodo. She put her hand over the floor and the same thing occurred. 'I can do it too,' she said.

Steven shook his head anxiously. 'The Doctor's game won't wait for us. We'll just have to take a chance.' As he spoke, from behind through the passageway, Sergeant Rugg and Mrs Wiggs emerged. Their clothes were now clean and beautifully fresh and pressed. They walked a little stiffly, even proudly.

'Hello,' said Dodo. 'You've made it up then.'

The Sergeant drew himself up to his full height once again. 'Mrs Wiggs has too warm a heart to keep a quarrel going.'

Mrs Wiggs giggled like a young girl. 'The Sergeant is going to take me to the ball.'

'The ball?' queried Dodo.

'Right in 'ere gel,' said the Sergeant. 'There's no lack of partners as you see.' He pointed over to the waiting dolls. 'They never get tired of dancing, them dollies.'

Steven, meanwhile, had been walking around the edge of the dance floor. The only way to reach the TARDIS was by crossing it. Without waiting further, Steven started striding across the floor. The music started. To his horror, Steven suddenly found himself dancing around to the steps of a Viennese waltz.

'It's no time for a dance, Steven,' said Dodo, laughing.

Steven looked back, his face stricken: 'I can't help myself.' Steven tried to get toward the edge of the floor, but every time he got near, he found himself whisked away as though he were on some invisible, moving turntable.

'Look out!' said Dodo anxiously. She pointed behind Steven and as he twirled around, he saw the three dolls move mechanically towards him.

The scene on the dance floor was being watched by the Toymaker in his private office. The tally recorder now read number 876 and the Doctor's hand was still visible, moving the counters from one place to another.

'You're doing very well, Doctor,' said the Toymaker. 'Let's hope you haven't made a mistake. But you'll find that out when you reach your 1023rd move.'

The Toymaker waved his hand lazily towards the screen. 'I see that Steven has taken some time off from the quest to go dancing.'

The hand stopped as if the invisible Doctor was watching the screen. 'Keep on playing,' said the Toymaker. 'Keep on playing.'

One of the ballerina dolls approached Steven, grabbed him around the waist and held his hand. It started to dance with him.

'Get away from it,' said Dodo. 'You must. The riddle warned us that if you started dancing it would be forever.'

Steven shook his head, sweat pouring from his brow. 'I can't,' he said. 'It's holding me here like steel! Don't come on to the floor, Dodo. Get back.'

'But then we can't reach the TARDIS,' said Dodo

97

anxiously.

'Perhaps I'll be able to move the doll nearer to it,' he said.

And even as he spoke, the doll guided Steven's feet effortlessly – further away from the TARDIS.

The Sergeant looked over at them: 'Not a bad dancer. For a civilian that is! And not a bad-looking couple.'

Mrs Wiggs turned to Dodo. 'He'd make a nicer partner for you, ducks.'

Dodo came to a sudden resolution. 'I'm going to try and reach the TARDIS,' she said. She jumped onto the dance floor and at once, she found herself dancing too.

Now the rhythm changed to a fast beat number. The doll disengaged Steven and started gyrating in front of him and Steven found himself tossing and turning on the dance floor to some disco beat. He turned and to his horror saw Dodo also on the floor dancing opposite a male ballet dancer doll. 'What are you doing?' he cried. 'Get away Dodo. Get back.'

Dodo shook her head. 'I can't,' she said.

Standing beside the dance floor, the Sergeant turned to Mrs Wiggs. 'Now we got them both dancing,' he said. 'What was it the Toymaker wanted us to do?'

Mrs Wiggs pointed over to the TARDIS: 'Reach that big cupboard before them.'

'And what about that other doll?' asked the Sergeant.

'Well, that's the game, ducks, ain't it? You dance with 'er and I'll run for the cupboard.'

'Begging your pardon, mum. This is men's work. You dance and I'll run.' Mrs Wiggs shook her head obstinately. The Sergeant continued. 'To be quite frank with you, missus, soldiers don't dance well, officers perhaps, but *never* sergeants! Now, why don't you try that floor?'

A little reluctantly, Mrs Wiggs stepped onto the dance floor and, as she did, the dolls changed partners. Steven's doll went to dance with Dodo; Dodo's doll went to dance with Mrs Wiggs; and the third doll came over to dance with Steven.

Steven, this time swept up in a 1920s tango rhythm and holding his partner around the waist, called to Dodo. 'Try and keep near me,' he said.

'Why?' said Dodo.

Steven shook his head at her. 'Tell you later.'

Mrs Wiggs, being swept around by her doll in long sweeping tango steps, was getting out of breath. 'I can't keep this up for long Sergeant,' she said. 'Go on, run for the cupboard.'

The Sergeant, who seemed reluctant to step on the dance floor, braced himself. 'Just on my way, Mrs W,' he said. He took a big stride onto the dance floor only to find that his feet weren't his own. He started to dance too. The music changed again – this time it was a snappy fox trot of the 1930s.

Once again the dolls changed partners. One of the ballerinas attached herself to the Sergeant. The male doll left Mrs Wiggs and took Dodo in his arms and Steven's doll approached Mrs Wiggs and started dancing. Just as Steven had hoped, he found himself unattached.

'Help,' said the Sergeant. 'What's happening?'

'I'm surprised at you, Sergeant Rugg,' said Mrs Wiggs. 'Put that hussy down and get to the cupboard.'

'I can't!' shouted the Sergeant.

Meanwhile, Steven said to Dodo. 'Keep going. Try to get as near as you can to the TARDIS. We're almost there, now concentrate. Now! Quick!'

By a great effort of will, Steven managed to steer himself as close as he could to the TARDIS. He reached forward, grabbed the door, pulled it open, turned, and as Dodo and her partner came past, grabbed her by the arm and pulled. Both of them shot inside and the door shut behind them.

For a moment, Dodo and Steven were too busy trying to catch their breath to take in their surroundings. Then they realised that they were in yet another police box.

'Another fake! I wonder how many of these things the Toymaker has.'

'Far too many,' said Dodo. 'I'm beginning to wonder if we'll ever find the real one at all.'

'Of course we will,' said Steven. 'Don't lose heart. We've been through too much.'

'I wonder if we'll ever see the sergeant and the cook again. They were rather nice you know,' said Dodo.

Steven shook his head in disbelief. 'You still believe in these creations of the Toymaker, don't you?' he said. 'You can't see that they are just phantoms – things created in his mind.'

'If that's so,' said Dodo. 'Why do they lose to us? And always through something silly and, yes, human, and in a way rather touching.'

Steven shook his head puzzled. 'I don't know,' he said. 'Perhaps they get out of his control.'

'There,' she said. Dodo always liked winning the argument when she could. 'That's what I meant.'

'Come again?' said Steven.

'He can bring them to life,' she explained. 'But they have wills and minds of their own. I'll never be able to look at a doll or a playing card again with an easy mind. They really live a secret life.'

Steven looked at her with concern as though she had flipped her lid this time, as he would have put it. 'We'd better get you out of this – and quickly.'

'What do you mean?' said Dodo, a bit annoyed.

'This place is beginning to get to you, isn't it?'

'Rubbish,' said Dodo, really annoyed now. 'Just because you can't see ...'

'Oh, come on,' said Steven. 'We'd better find the next clue.'

Back in the study, the Toymaker was watching the screen. He saw the Sergeant and Mrs Wiggs, now dancing together, get smaller and smaller, reverting to their doll's size. The Toymaker waved his arm angrily and the screen became blank. He then turned to the Doctor.

'You dare to laugh at me, do you, Doctor? You forget I can see you when no-one else can. You laugh too soon. The game is not yet over – either for you or your clever friends. They still have another game or two to play, and they mustn't win this next game.'

The Toymaker strode quickly over to the doll's house and surveyed a small row of dolls. There were the clowns, the playing cards, and the Sergeant and Cook dolls laid out.

'I was foolish to trust you to play my games,' said the Toymaker. He turned and opened a chest and threw the dolls inside carelessly. 'Clowns! Playing cards! Nursery characters! All too human and too kind. No. This time I must find a more deadly opponent.' He turned around and, from the doll's house, brought out the figure of a round, rather fat, English schoolboy in school uniform – cap, blazer, short trousers, long socks and leather shoes.

He held it up and looked at it. 'The most deadly opponent of all,' he said, 'because he appears the most innocent. A fat, jolly, school boy: who could suspect him? My friend Cyril!' He laughed. 'I wonder what your friends will make of him, Doctor?'

He looked over at the tally recorder which now registered 899. As he watched, it clicked on to 900. 'You only have 123 moves to go, Doctor,' he said. 'I think we've got you this time.'

Back in the fake TARDIS, Steven was beginning to get frustrated. 'Can you see any way out of this?' he asked. 'We can't go back in on the dance floor.' He started to push at one of the walls but nothing happened.

'What do you think that is?' said Dodo. She pointed to one of the three walls on which was marked a large arrow pointing up to the roof of the police box. The words *Start Here* were written alongside the arrow. Steven reached up and started examining the wall on which the arrow was painted. Further up, there was a piece of paper at the tip of the arrow. He reached up and got it.

'This must be the next riddle,' he said. As soon as he had ripped the paper off the wall, the wall slowly descended until it was flat upon the ground and revealed a passageway – dark at the entrance but with a distant glimmer of light at the end.

'I don't like the look of it,' said Steven.

'Nevertheless,' said Dodo, 'we'd better go down there.'

'Hold on,' said Steven. 'Just a minute. Let's see what this says.' He opened up the piece of paper and read the words written on it: *Lady luck will show the way; win the game, or here you'll stay.*

'That's much shorter than the others were,' said Dodo.

'That doesn't mean it will be any easier,' said Steven. 'Come on.' He started to lead the way down the passage. As they walked down towards the end, the light became gradually brighter and brighter until it almost dazzled them.

'I can hardly see,' said Dodo.

'Wait a for a minute before we enter this,' said Steven.

Dodo slowly opened her eyes against the glare, then screamed. There was a strange figure standing in front of them.

Cryil was standing in school boy's uniform but with the knave's hat on. As they watched, he took it off, then put on the kitchen boy's chef's hat. Then he took the chef's hat off and replaced it with a school cap. He leered at them out of the corner of his mouth.

'Who are you?' said Steven. 'We've seen you before, haven't we?'

'I'm Cyril. I was the Knave and the kitchen boy, so we're old friends, aren't we? Huh, I had you that time. Did I scare you?'

'You certainly did, Cyril,' said Dodo indignantly.

'Let's be friends,' said Cyril. He offered his gloved hand to Steven who shook it and jumped back.

'Oh!' cried Steven. He shook his hand. 'I got a shock. He must have some sort of a electrical device there.' Cyril's fat body was shaking with laughter.

'You should see your face,' said Cyril.

'You'll feel my hand in a moment,' said Steven. 'What have you got there?' he grabbed Cyril's arm and dragged back his sleeve to reveal two wires and a small battery strapped to his wrist.

'I say,' said Cyril. 'Careful! I'll show you.' He stripped his glove off and showed the rubber-backed electrode which gave Steven the shock.

'Take that thing off,' said Steven. Cyril took the glove off and untaped the battery on his wrist.

'There you are,' said Cyril.

'Have you any more of these silly schoolboy jokes on you?' queried Steven.

Cyril looked sulky. 'No,' he said. 'I don't know why you're taking on like this. I've come to be friends with you.'

'Charming way you have to make friends,' said Steven.

Dodo was always ready to be sympathetic, 'He didn't mean any harm,' she said. 'Did you?'

Cyril nodded eagerly. 'Oh no,' he said. He pulled a somewhat grubby bag of sweets from his pocket and offered them to her. 'Have one of these,' he said.

Dodo shook her head. 'No, thanks,' she said.

'Oh go on,' he said. 'They're quite harmless. They're humbugs.' Again, Dodo shook her head but Steven nudged her.

'Take them, Dodo, or we'll be here all day.' Dodo took the sweets and put them away in her pocket.

'Thank you,' said Cyril. 'If I eat any more, I'll be sick, I suspect.' He turned to Steven. 'You're my hero, you know,' he said. 'I want to grow up just like you.'

'*When* you grow up?' said Steven puzzled. Cyril nodded his head. 'You look pretty grown up already to me.'

Dodo, meanwhile, had been looking off at the Doctor's tally screen. 'Steven!' she interjected. 'The Doctor's reached move 902.'

Steven nodded. 'We'd better hurry then. Where's the game we have to play?' he asked Cyril.

'Oh, right over there,' said Cyril. 'You won't have such an easy time of it for your next game, because you're going to be playing against me.'

He turned to face them and for a moment, his round face with big blue eyes showed an expression of almost devilish cunning that made Steven and Dodo draw back from him.

9

The Final Test

'It looks like a huge pinball machine,' said Dodo
excitedly. The reason for the glare as they had come out
of the dark passage was now apparent. They were
confronted by a room in which the ceiling, the walls and
the floor were illuminated from behind. On the lighted
floor was a series of triangles like the ones found on
arcade pinball machines. These were also lighted up in
different colours. The triangles were numbered one to
fourteen. Triangle fourteen was much bigger than the
others and had the word *Home* flashing on the top. The
numbered triangles led in a twisting snake-like fashion
around the room before ending up on the home triangle.

'This looks much easier than the other games,' said
Dodo. She turned to Cyril. For answer, Cyril bent down
and opened up a school satchel he had left lying on the
floor. From the satchel he brought a large dice and a dice
shaker, placing them on the floor near the first triangle
marked *Start*.

'Here's the dice,' said Cyril. 'When it's your turn to
move, throw it and the number will show on the
indicator over there.' Cyril pointed over to the back of
the room where there was yet another TARDIS. Beside
it, was a large cylinder, like a barber's pole with bright
red, white and blue stripes. It was turning slowly and, as

it turned, a message formed on the side. The riddle became visible. *Lady Luck will show the way, win the game, or here you'll stay.*

'You move forward the same number of triangles as the number shown on the dice. It's really very simple: the first one to reach triangle fourteen' – he pointed over to the *Home* triangle, – is the winner!'

'It's almost *too* easy,' said Steven. 'What's the catch?'

'No catch,' said Cyril, looking blandly from one to the other with his large, blue eyes. 'First home is the winner.'

'I still don't understand.' Steven shook his head. 'That gives us a two to one chance over you.'

'Oh,' said Cyril. His blue eyes grew even wider and more deceptively innocent-looking. 'Why, so it does. But there it is. I shall just have to put up with it, won't I? We shall all jump from one triangle to another and the one who gets there, *Home*, is the winner.'

'Why jump?' asked Steven. 'Why can't we just walk on the floor from one triangle to another?'

'Oh,' said Cyril. 'Of course, you can walk if you like, but I shouldn't if I were you.'

'Why not?' asked Dodo.

'Because after triangle number four all the area between the spaces is electrified and you'll be killed.' Cyril's face creased into an entirely cherubic little smile as his eyes flicked from Dodo to Steven.

In the Toymaker's private office, the Toymaker, with his hands folded mandarin style, was gloating to the Doctor. 'I don't think your friends will do so well now,

Doctor. Cyril hates to lose, so he makes sure he never does.'

The Doctor's hand hesitated. Above them the tally recorder flashed the move 905.

'Oh, please don't stop playing,' said the Toymaker. 'You're so near the end now. Soon we'll discover whether or not you got the sequence right.'

'Right now you need help.' The Toymaker raised his voice to the high-pitched sound he used to give commands to the trilogic game. 'Go from move 930.' Immediately there was a clicking noise and the pieces started flying across the board of their own volition until the tally indicator clicked up to 930.

'There,' said the Toymaker. 'At this rate, you'll finish long before Dodo and Steven reach the TARDIS. And you'll have to stay here. You know, your two friends will make such charming dolls. Look over here.'

The Toymaker walked over to the doll's house and opened it. 'Look, two chairs, all ready and waiting for them. And here, I've had some special costumes made for when they play games.' The Toymaker opened a tiny wardrobe and pulled out two intricately crafted Victorian children's suits. 'They'll be companions for Cyril. The poor boy gets very lonely at times.'

Steve and Dodo were now ready to start the game.

'Ready?' said Cyril. 'Jolly good show. Now, you know what to do?' Dodo and Steven nodded.

'Right ho then, ladies first.' He bowed to Dodo who took up the shaker and threw the dice onto the nearest triangle; it showed a three. Counting from the start triangle, she hopped a little unsteadily over to triangle four.

Cyril turned to Steven. 'You next,' he said.

Steven looked at him suspiciously. 'You're just too good to be true, you are,' he said. Cyril gave another bland cherubic smile and Steven threw the dice and got a four. Hopping past Dodo, he landed on triangle number five.

A buzzer sounded. Steven looked around: there on the indicator, the letters resolved themselves into a direction which said, *Move forward two paces.*

Steven turned back to Cyril. 'It said move forward two paces. Do I?'

'Oh, you are a lucky chap,' said Cyril. 'Yes, go on to number seven.'

'Oh, one thing I didn't tell you by the way,' Cyril called as Steven hopped two more paces to land on number seven. 'When a player lands on an occupied triangle, the first player has to go back to the starting post.'

'Great,' said Steven to Dodo. 'Now I see why he let us go first. Well, go on them. Don't keep us in suspense.'

Cyril took the dice shaker and threw a two. He grimaced and jumped two squares to square three.

'My turn now,' said Dodo. She reached over and took the dice from Cyril and threw herself a three. 'Look,' she said to Steven. 'I've got a –' As the implications of the number three sank in, her face fell. 'Oh, dear,' she said. 'That means I'll be coming on your square, Steven.'

Steven turned back to Cyril. 'Surely we can't send each other home,' he queried. 'We're playing together.'

'Those are the rules,' said Cyril a little smugly. 'You'll

never win if you don't follow them.'

Dodo jumped on to Steven's square. 'He's right, Steven,' she said. 'We must play fair. We are two to one, after all.'

Steven nodded a little ungraciously. 'All right. But keep an eye on him.' He hopped from triangle to triangle back to the start. When he landed on the start triangle, it lighted up with the words *Miss a turn*.

Steven looked down in dismay. 'What does this mean?' he queried.

Cyril turned to Dodo laughing. 'He's pretending he doesn't know how to play,' he said. 'What a sense of humour.' He turned back to Steven. 'It means you miss your next turn. It's all part of the game. It's my turn now.' Taking the dice, he threw a three as the other two looked at him suspiciously.

'Oh, a three. I'm still just behind you,' he said to Dodo. Dodo nodded and turned back towards where the robot had now appeared with the chest screen showing the Doctor's progress in the trilogic game.

'Look, Steven,' she said. 'The robot again. And it's got the Doctor's score on it. The Doctor's reached 950. We'll have to hurry.'

She turned back again and gave a scream, staggering and almost falling off her triangle. Someone with a hideous mask was leering at her. The mask dropped and Cyril was revealed.

'It's only me, Cyril,' said the schoolboy. Steven jumped over to join them.

'I told you about those idiotic jokes,' he said threateningly. 'She nearly fell off.'

Cyril laughed. 'All in the game, old chap. Now, you

both go back to the start. You've broken the rules by coming here.'

'That's not fair,' said Dodo.

'He cheated,' said Cyril. 'Moved ahead when it wasn't his turn. Now he must go back to the start. I've landed on your square.' He turned to Dodo. 'So back you both go.'

Steven's patience reached its limit. 'I've had enough of this,' he said. 'You make the rules up as you go along. Come on, Dodo, we'll go to the finish and see if that's the real TARDIS.' Steven turned and hopped on the next triangle moving towards the Home triangle with the TARDIS behind it.

There was a thunderclap and the Toymaker appeared on the next triangle. 'Don't you like my little game?' he asked.

Steven stopped short,' startled for a moment, then he shook his head. 'No, I don't,' he said.

'What a pity,' said the Toymaker. 'To give up now after having overcome so many obstacles.'

Dodo shook her head: 'We're not giving up.'

'Are you sure?' asked the Toymaker. 'It sounded like it.'

'I must get to the end of this,' said Steven. He tried to get past the Toymaker but seemed to bang up against some invisible wall. He reached his hand out – there was something blocking the way.

'It's no use,' he said. 'There's some sort of invisible barrier here.'

'Precisely,' said the Toymaker. 'A barrier that yields only to those who play fairly. Those are the rules. Now perhaps you will go back to the starting platform as requested.' The Toymaker gave one of his slow smiles and vanished.

Steven stared after him for a moment, then turned back to Dodo. 'Come on, Dodo,' he said. They went back to the beginning.

As Steven landed on number four, something hit him a sharp stinging blow on the back of his neck. He teetered for a moment, raising his hand at the sting and nearly fell.

'Ouch,' he said. 'What on earth was that?' He turned around. Cyril was putting a catapult away in his pocket.

'Hurrah!' said Cyril. 'One up for me. Now it's my turn.' He threw a two with the dice and advanced two more triangles.

Steven rejoined Dodo on the start triangle. 'I'm going to see if there is any barrier around his back side,' he said.

'Oh don't,' said Dodo. 'Whose turn is it?'

'Mine,' said Steven. He rolled the dice shaker and got a six. 'That's better.' He looked up and called across to Cyril. 'Do I get a second turn for a six?'

Cyril looked down his nose. 'Certainly not!' he said.

Steven nodded dryly. He was beginning to get the hang of this game. 'I thought not somehow,' he said.

In the Toymaker's office, the Toymaker smiled at the invisible Doctor. 'I've had to speak to your friends, Doctor,' he said. 'It seems they do not know how to play a game fairly. But don't worry, Cyril seems to have the game nicely in hand. I don't think your friends are going to get the TARDIS back. As you are certain to lose, I feel I should be kinder to you.' He clicked his fingers. 'There, I've given you back your voice. You are no longer under the ban of silence.'

The Doctor's hand continued to move above the trilogic board. The tally recorder registered 960.

'Now you're sulking,' said the Toymaker irritated. 'Have you forgotten how to speak?'

For a moment the hand hesitated, then the Doctor's voice came out clear. 'Throughout the game,' said the Doctor, 'you have done everything in your power to break my concentration. It is very unlikely that you will succeed now.'

'Perhaps this will alter your concentration,' said the Toymaker. 'Look, Doctor.' He pointed over to the screen and the picture reappeared. 'Your friend Steven has had to miss a turn.'

Back in the toyroom, Steven had just landed on a triangle near the middle of the game with Dodo two triangles behind him and Cyril now only four from the finish line. Steven's triangle read *Miss a turn*.

Cyril turned back smugly. 'You haven't a hope of beating me now! Why don't you both give up? I only need a three to win.'

Steven ignored him and turned to Dodo. 'It's up to you now,' he said. Dodo shook her dice shaker and brought out the dice watched eagerly by Steven.

Neither of them saw Cyril bring out a packet of powder and carefully spread it over most of the triangle on which he was standing. He stealthily tried a foot on it. The foot slid towards the edge. He drew it back and smiled.

'Look,' said Dodo. 'A six!' She started jumping on the triangles until she was up to the square behind Cyril. 'I only need a four to get home now,' she said.

Cyril looked even more sulky. He was fast losing his cherubic quality. His blue eyes now looked hard and cold. 'But it's my turn first,' he said pouting. 'Too bad, isn't it?'

He threw his dice and it showed a two. Then he hopped forward two paces. The triangle lighted up with the message *Go back four paces*.

Cyril looked around quickly at the other two. Steven and Dodo were watching the counter on the trilogic game which had now gone up to 980. Cyril bent down, trying to block the message with his body while he tied his shoelace. But Dodo caught him out of the corner of her eye.

'Steven, look,' she said. 'He has to go back four paces.'

'Now who's trying to cheat?' said Steven.

'Give a chap time to tie his shoelace,' said the schoolboy. He straightened up and sulkily jumped back past Dodo, being very careful to land on the unslippery part of the triangle onto which he had put the powder.

'That's better,' said Steven. 'Go on, Dodo, you must get a four.' Dodo took the dice shaker up and shook it only to be interrupted by a howl of agony. She turned back quickly. Cyril was lying over the triangle with one foot dangling over the edge. As she watched he brought it up and she could see blood soaking his stocking.

'He's hurt himself,' said Dodo.

Steven shook his head. 'It's a trick. Throw the dice,'

he said.

Cyril's shrieks got worse. He pulled his shoes off and Dodo saw that his entire sock was soaked with blood.

'He's bleeding,' said Dodo. 'His foot must have slipped off and touched the floor. He's really hurt badly, Steven. We can't just leave him there.

'Go ahead and play!' said Steven urgently.

'No,' said Dodo. 'I'm going to help him.' Dodo jumped back to Cyril's square and immediately bent down to examine his foot. 'Where does it hurt?' she said concerned. 'We'd better take your sock off.' She started pulling it and then looked at her hands. 'This isn't blood,' she said. 'It's red ink.'

'Of course it is,' said Cyril rudely. 'You're too easy to fool. Now you can just go back to the beginning and miss a turn for leaving your triangle.' He jumped up in his stocking feet. 'That makes it my turn again.'

Dodo was outraged. 'Well,' she said. 'Of all the spiteful things.'

'Teach you to think you can beat me in a game.' He rolled his dice and threw a five. 'A five!' he said. He quickly counted the spaces to home. 'Look! I've won. I'm the winner!'

In his excitement, Cyril left his shoes standing where they were. He immediately starting jumping the triangles back towards the home base and the TARDIS. In his haste, he forgot the trap he had prepared for the others. His stockinged feet landed on the slippery part of the triangle. He desperately tried to keep his balance – his arms flailing, but it was no use. He shot over the edge of the triangle and landed with a crash on the electrified floor. There was a shriek, a puff of smoke and then silence.

Immediately all the lights on the triangles began flashing on and off. The room began to darken.

'What's happened?' asked a frightened Dodo.

Leaving his triangle, Steven came over to join her. 'I don't know,' he said. He jumped over to Cyril's last triangle, slipped but managed to regain his balance. He leant down and felt the slippery dancehall chalk powder that Cyril had placed on the triangle.

'Careful, Dodo,' he said. Dodo came up and carefully eased herself down beside Steven on the triangle. 'Look,' he said. 'It's covered with some kind of slippery powder. He must have put it on and then forgotten about it in the excitement. Serves him right. He was caught in his own trap.' He looked over. Where Cyril had fallen, there was merely a charred doll.

'Come on, Dodo,' said Steven. 'The game's over now.'

Dodo shook her head. 'No we'd better play the game to the end. You heard what the Toymaker said. I'm sure I can throw that four.' She took up the dice and closed her eyes in concentration.

'Dodo,' said Steven urgently. 'Look at the tally.'

Dodo glanced over at the robot. The tally now read 1014.

'The Doctor has nearly finished his game,' said Steven.

Dodo rolled the dice. It showed a four. 'We've won, Steven!'

'Quickly then, jump!' In a blaze of flashing lights, the pair jumped over the remaining triangles to reach home base. As soon as they arrived, the flashing lights stopped and the lighting came back to normal. They turned towards the TARDIS. Steven put his hand out to the door and shook it but it was locked.

'Do you suppose it's the real one this time?' asked Dodo.

Steven listened. 'I think so. Listen, it hums. The others didn't hum, remember.'

Dodo shook her head. 'It still doesn't mean it's the TARDIS,' she said. 'After all our hard work.' She lent despondently against the door. Steven snapped his fingers.

'Of course!' he said. 'The Doctor's still got the key. He will have to finish his game first to come here to let us in.'

He turned to look back at the board. The tally now read 1022.

10

Stalemate

His game nearly completed, the Doctor suddenly found himself completely visible again.

He was looking up at the screen, having watched Steven and Dodo successfully complete their game. 'There,' he said tapping his lapel. 'I was right.'

The Toymaker, quieter than before, was sitting opposite him, watching the Doctor, with his snake-like eyes. 'Make the last move, Doctor,' he said.

The Doctor thought for a moment. 'Aha, no,' he said. 'Not for a moment. I see that Dodo and Steven have found the TARDIS. The moment they touched it, your childish trick was broken – I'm visible again. Now you have to let us go.'

'You are indeed visible,' said the Toymaker. 'And you've done very well. The three of you have won my little game.'

The Doctor turned and looked at him, a little caustically. 'I'm so glad you take it so calmly,' he said. 'And now if you'll excuse me, I'd like to make sure the TARDIS is all right.' The Doctor got up, walked over to the wall, part of which immediately slid away, and passing through, he found himself in the game room with Steven and Dodo.

Dodo and Steven had their backs to the Doctor and

were trying to open the door.

'Are you sure the Toymaker couldn't have made a TARDIS hum like this one?' said Dodo.

'If he could have done that,' said Steven, 'why didn't he make the other ones hum too.'

'Well done, my boy,' the Doctor's familiar voice sounded behind them. 'I'm glad you're starting to put logic into your guesses.' Steven and Dodo whirled around.

'Doctor,' cried Dodo, 'you're safe.' In tears, she ran over and hugged him. 'You've won your game.'

'Yes, yes,' said the Doctor. 'Well done, both of you. Well now, it's time to be off. He crossed over, brought a key out from his pocket and opened the door of the TARDIS.

'I certainly can't wait to leave this place,' said Steven. 'I hope I don't have to play another game ever!'

The Doctor twinkled back at him. 'I don't think you'll have to, my boy.'

Abruptly the Toymaker appeared beside them. 'I hope I do not interrupt your counsel of war,' said the Toymaker.

'Do not waste our time on trivial formalities,' said the Doctor. 'You have been defeated. Leave us alone.'

'Yes,' said Dodo. 'You knew you must lose in the end.'

The Toymaker laughed at her. 'Oh, but you're so wrong. Only I can win. If I lose, the Doctor and I go down together. Isn't that so, Doctor?'

'Go away, you charlatan,' said the Doctor.

'Ah,' said the Toymaker. 'Go on, young people, ask your elderly friend if he can win completely.'

Steven turned around to look at the Doctor. 'Is it true, Doctor? Are we bound to fail?'

The Doctor shook his head. 'No,' he said. 'He's trying to trick us into despair. Don't listen to him.'

'Tell the truth,' the Toymaker insisted. 'Go ahead, Doctor. Hide nothing!'

Dodo looked anxious. 'You must tell us what you know, Doctor. We have a right.'

Finally the Doctor nodded. 'Very well,' he said. 'I am compelled to tell the truth. Even though we have won, there is still a chance the Toymaker can drag us down in defeat with him. Unless ...'

'Unless,' Steven cocked his eyebrows.

'It's a question of timing,' said the Doctor.

'Oh please, Doctor,' said Dodo. 'Tell us, do we have a chance to escape?'

'Yes,' said the Doctor. 'We have a chance but we have to proceed very carefully.'

The Toymaker smiled. 'An impossible chance,' he said.

Steven broke in angrily. 'As long as we defeat you, that's all I care about. You can't beat us now.'

The Doctor turned and nodded approvingly to Steven. 'Well said my boy.'

'Well said?' rejoined the Toymaker. 'Does he know what he's saying? Remember the past: remember my power.'

That was too much for Steven. Angered he turned on the Toymaker. 'We won,' he said. 'You just won't acknowledge it.'

'Well perhaps you'd like to go through those little adventures again. And –'

Steven lunged forward at the Toymaker. 'Not before I lay my hands on you,' he said. The Toymaker stood quite still, but Steven, acting as though he was being violently manhandled, fell back, landing with a smack on the hard floor.

The Doctor helped Steven to his feet. 'It's no use, leave him alone.'

Steven said a little breathlessly, 'I can't touch him?'

The Doctor shook his head. 'He's using his mind to turn your own physical energy against yourself.' He waved the other two into the TARDIS. 'Go on,' he said. 'Inside. I'll deal with him.'

'I really don't know why you want to leave here, Doctor.' The Toymaker's tone was most conciliatory now. 'There will always be a toymaker in the world ready to make more and more inventive machines. That is, until one is made that will destroy his world. But each time, the world can be recreated and we can have the fun of building better and better toys. Why not join me, Doctor?'

The Doctor stared at him for a moment. 'I won't join you,' he said, 'because you and your kind are evil. The toys you make have no use except to amuse yourselves and ultimately lead to your own destruction. Toys should be left in the nursery where they belong, not decide the fate of worlds. You have failed.'

He turned, ran into the TARDIS and slammed the door behind him.

The Toymaker looked after the Doctor for a moment, his face blank and enigmatic. Then he smiled, laughed to himself, turned and waved his hand. The trilogic game appeared before him with two chairs. Taking his time, the Toymaker carefully sat down in one and rearranged his heavy, jewel-encrusted Mandarin's gown around him. 'We shall see, old man, we shall see ...'

There was a brief pause, and then, as the Toymaker had expected, the Doctor slowly emerged from the TARDIS and came over to him. He was furious.

'What have you done?' said the Doctor. 'How dare you meddle with my machine!'

'It isn't what I have done,' said the Toymaker. 'It's what you haven't. You must finish the game. You cannot leave until you've finished it.'

The Doctor crossed to the trilogic game and looked down at it. 'Your infantile behaviour is beyond a joke,' he said. He raised his hand to pick up the last piece and then froze, remembering.

'No,' he said. 'No, I mustn't!' He pointed at the Toymaker. 'You nearly caught me that time, didn't you?'

The Toymaker shrugged. 'Make your move, Doctor,' he said.

The Doctor shook his head. 'If I do so, then this place vanishes.'

The Toymaker nodded. 'Yes, you will have really won.'

'If this place vanishes, then the TARDIS and the rest of us will vanish with it,' said the Doctor.

The Toymaker smiled a self-satisfied smile. 'Correct. That is the price of success. Make your last move, Doctor. Make your *last* move.'

★

Inside the TARDIS, Dodo and Steven were waiting anxiously for the Doctor. 'What can be keeping him?' said Steven.

Dodo shook her head. 'Something the Toymaker has done to the TARDIS. The Doctor has to persuade the Toymaker to let us go, I think.'

Steven looked crossly at Dodo. 'We won his games, so we have the right to go. The Doctor said so.'

Dodo shivered. 'Well, as long as I'm safely inside here, I don't mind so much.'

They turned as the Doctor came in. For the first time, he was looking worried and a little tired. He crossed over to the console and started to manipulate certain controls, then pressed a button. Nothing happened. He shook his head. 'It's no use,' he said.

'What's happened?' queried Steven. 'What has he done?'

'By beating the Toymaker we shall destroy this world.'

'What's wrong with that?' said Steven.

'Surely, that's a very good thing. This is such a sad place,' said Dodo.

'You don't understand,' said the Doctor. 'As soon as the games are over and won, the Toymaker's whole world vanishes and, as we are still trapped inside his world, we will vanish with him. We will become non-matter.'

'But we have won,' Dodo cried. 'It hasn't happened yet.'

'It will the moment I go out there and make the final move on the trilogic game.'

'Why doesn't he just let us go?' said Steven pacing up

and down inside the TARDIS. 'He can't want to be destroyed.'

The Doctor shook his head. 'He won't be.'

'If everything disappears, then why not him?' queried Dodo.

'If he loses the game,' said the Doctor, 'then his world vanishes. He doesn't. And he has the power to build a new one.'

'How?' said Dodo.

'All toymakers are immortal,' said the Doctor. 'The urge to create toys that are ultimately destructive is unfortunately part of our universe. This Toymaker's lasted for thousands of years. Vey occasionally he loses one of his games, then he has to pay the price.'

'And that price,' said Steven, 'is the loss of his world?'

The Doctor nodded. 'But he himself is not destroyed; he goes on forever.'

'Then we can't leave,' said Steven.

'There must be a way.' The Doctor turned back to the control panel and turned on the scanner. They could see the Toymaker sitting beside the trilogic board patiently waiting for them.

Then, as they watched, he came over close to the scanner and started touching the TARDIS, admiring it. He tried the door, found it locked and smiled.

The Doctor turned, and called into the microphone. 'Will you leave my ship alone!' he said.

'Oh, do let me have it, Doctor,' said the Toymaker. 'You must admit, we've reached a stalemate now, and it would be *such* an amusing toy. You might as well give up and join me.'

'Let me bring the trilogic board inside here,' said the

Doctor.

The Toymaker thought for a moment, then smiled. 'You must think me very naïve, Doctor. I see your ploy. If you can make the final move in there, then you can preset your controls and dematerialise at the same moment as my world vanishes. Then you'll get away from me.'

'That will make no difference to you,' said the Doctor. 'You can make a new world.'

'Well, of course I can,' said the Toymaker. 'And I'm looking forward to that. I was rather tired of this one. But, I'm such a bad loser, Doctor. I *always* destroy the destroyer of my world.'

'I will not come out and make that move,' said the Doctor firmly.

The Toymaker smiled once more. 'Then you will stay there forever.'

Steven came to a resolution and walked up to the Doctor. 'Let me go out,' he said. 'I'll make the last move for you.'

The Doctor shook his head. 'Nonesense, my boy. You don't want to disappear.'

'At least you two can get away safely.'

The Doctor looked at his companion for a moment, moved. 'That's very kind of you but I absolutely forbid it. You have done more than enough to get the TARDIS back.'

'Well, something's got to be done,' said Steven. 'We can't just sit here and talk our way out of this place.'

The Doctor wheeled on him, his eyes flashing. 'Of course!' he shouted. 'That's just what we can do! Talk our way out of here!'

For a moment Steven and Dodo stared at the Doctor wondering if he had lost his wits. Then the Doctor turned around, speaking into the TARDIS's microphone. 'Listen to me,' he said. 'I *will* make the final move.'

The Toymaker turned around to face the scanner and smiled a smile of triumph. 'How sensible of you,' he said.

'Go back over to the trilogic table and take your seat there,' said the Doctor.

The Toymaker smiled, shrugged his shoulders, and then walked over and sat down by the table. 'Are you ready?' asked the Doctor.

'Whenever you are, Doctor,' replied the Toymaker.

'Very well. Go to move 1023,' he said into the microphone.

Nothing happened.

The Doctor frowned, then his face cleared. This time, he pitched his voice high, imitating the high sharp tone the Toymaker had used when he had issued his directions to make the pieces move round the board in the trilogic game: 'Go to move 1023.'

Taken entirely my surprise, the Toymaker glanced quickly at the board. The final piece rose up in the air and started moving over. He quickly brought his hand up to try and stop it, but it was too late. The piece hovered for a moment, then settled on the top of the triangle.

Inside the TARDIS, Steven was activating the controls at the split second the Doctor spoke. The familiar sound of the TARDIS dematerialising started up. The screen went black and then gradually resolved itself to the disintegration of a star. White clouds of debris flew in every direction. The Celestial Toyroom was no more.

Almost unable to believe their luck, Steven and Dodo shook their heads in astonishment. 'You did it!' said Dodo. 'You did it! We've got away!'

'Well done, Doctor,' said Steven. 'Well done. But how did you manage it?'

The Doctor turned back, looking very pleased with himself. 'Your idea, my boy,' he said. 'When the Toymaker wanted to move the pieces, he told them to move in a certain tone of voice, and they moved by themselves.'

'But you had to do it twice,' said Dodo.

'Ah, well,' said the Doctor. 'The first time didn't work because I used my own voice. The second time I remembered, and imitated the Toymaker's voice to make them obey me, and they did.'

'We'll never meet him again, will we, Doctor?' asked Dodo.

'Ah, I wish that was so,' said the Doctor. 'But the mind is indestructible and so is the Toymaker. I'm afraid the world is full of destructive toymakers like him.'

'Do you mean that he and his like can never be destroyed?' said Steven.

'Even though you defeated him?' said Dodo.

'This time yes, but there will be other meetings in other times,' said the Doctor. 'There will always be a Celestial Toyroom in the universe.'

THIS OFFER EXCLUSIVE TO

READERS

Pin up magnificent full colour posters of DOCTOR WHO

Just send £2.50 for the first poster and £1.25 for each additional poster

TO: PUBLICITY DEPARTMENT *
    W. H. ALLEN & CO PLC
    44 HILL STREET
    LONDON W1X 8LB

Cheques, Postal Orders made payable to WH Allen PLC

POSTER 1 ☐   POSTER 2 ☐   POSTER 3 ☐
POSTER 4 ☐   POSTER 5 ☐

Please allow 28 DAYS for delivery.

I enclose £ _____

CHEQUE NO. _____

ACCESS, VISA CARD NO. _____

Name _____

Address _____

_____

*For Australia, New Zealand, USA and Canada apply to distributors
listed on back cover for details and local price list